Praise for
The Simple Art of Flying

"Warmhearted, delightfully quirky, and believable."
—*KIRKUS REVIEWS*

"Reminiscent of *The One and Only* Ivan's
storytelling, Leonardo has crafted a tale that will
have readers rooting for each character ... A witty
animal-centered story that will remind readers that
families come in many shapes and sizes."
—*SLJ*

"This is a book about animals, friendship, and love,
but mostly about how everyone needs to be loved and
needed, whether they are an animal or a human."
—*SCHOOL LIBRARY CONNECTION*

THE SIMPLE ART OF FLYING

CORY LEONARDO

Aladdin

New York   London   Toronto   Sydney   New Delhi

ALADDIN
An imprint of Simon & Schuster Children's Publishing Division
1230 Avenue of the Americas, New York, New York 10020
First Aladdin paperback edition February 2020
Text copyright © 2019 by Cory Leonardo
Cover illustration copyright © 2019 by Jennifer Bricking
Also available in an Aladdin hardcover edition

For information about special discounts for bulk purchases, please contact Simon & Schuster Special Sales at 1-866-506-1949 or business@simonandschuster.com.
The Simon & Schuster Speakers Bureau can bring authors to your live event.
For more information or to book an event, contact the Simon & Schuster Speakers Bureau at 1-866-248-3049 or visit our website at www.simonspeakers.com.
Cover designed by Jessica Handelman and Nina Simoneaux
Interior designed by Mike Rosamilia
The text of this book was set in Adobe Caslon Pro.
Manufactured in the United States of America 0120 OFF
2 4 6 8 10 9 7 5 3 1
The Library of Congress has cataloged the hardcover edition as follows:
Names: Leonardo, Cory, author.
Title: The simple art of flying / by Cory Leonardo.
Description: First Aladdin hardcover edition. | New York : Aladdin, 2019. |
Summary: Alastair the African grey parrot is adopted by elderly dance-enthusiast and pie-baker Albertina Plopky and his sister, Aggie, by twelve-year-old Fritz, spoiling his plans to fly away with Aggie. Told in Alastair, Albertina, and Fritz's voices.
Identifiers: LCCN 2018023277 (print) | LCCN 2018029240 (eBook) |
ISBN 9781534421011 (eBook) | ISBN 9781534420991 (hardback)
Subjects: | CYAC: Pet adoption—Fiction. | Pet shops—Fiction. | African grey parrot—Fiction. |
Parrots—Fiction. | Friendship—Fiction. | Families—Fiction. | BISAC: JUVENILE
FICTION / Social Issues / Friendship. | JUVENILE FICTION / Family /
Alternative Family. | JUVENILE FICTION / Animals / Birds.
Classification: LCC PZ7.1.L468 (eBook) | LCC PZ7.1.L468 Sim 2019 (print) |
DDC [Fic]—dc23
LC record available at https://lccn.loc.gov/2018023277
ISBN 9781534421004 (pbk)

SOLI DEO GLORIA

A ~~Fish~~ Bird Story

"Call me Ishmael."[1]
I ate that sentence once
in a thick steak of a novel.
It wasn't my usual diet of
Frost, Whitman, Keats,
but it tasted all right anyway,
a little salty maybe, a smidge
fishy, but good.
I prefer the poetry, though.
Always have.
Since the first time I wrapped my
beak around the meat of a
Norton Anthology,[2] I was a
fish on a line—hooked.
When all your tongue has known
has been the blandness of
phone books, the sour snack of
tax forms, the cardboard-y flavor of
cardboard, that first bite of Shakespeare

---

1. "Call me Ishmael": famous first line of Herman Melville's *Moby-Dick*.
2. *Norton Anthology*: a particularly delectable book of poems.

is nectar, I tell you. Almost makes
a fella forget there are other books
to chew, the way it satisfies long.
And the act of remembering,
regurgitating—it fills the taste buds once more . . .

"Call me Ishmael."
I ate that sentence once and knew
it would come back to me to be savored again
if ever I set out to write my story.
And it has.
Just like the poems, it's come back,
filled my beak, taken flavors
old and new, same and
different.

I am a bird.
These are my poems.
This is my story.

Call me Alastair.

THE SIMPLE
ART OF FLYING

PART I

A TALE of TWO PARROTS
— OR —
GONE with the WING

CHAPTER 1

*Y*ou're born blind, so you only hear things at first. The crack of your shell. The whirring lullaby of the air around you. The muffled pips and peeps inside the two eggs nearby. You manage by a series of guesses those first few days. And without much else to go on, the things you *hear* stick with you.

It wasn't a few hours before I heard my first whopper of a tale—my first fish story.

"Alastair—that's you. *Psittacus erithacus erithacus.* Bird.

"And I'm Fritz. *Homo sapiens.* That's

Latin for 'wise man.' It just means I
have a bigger brain . . . and I'm top of
the food chain."

Right.

Apparently, I was born an African grey. A parrot.
A bird of small brains.

Doesn't sound suspicious at all.

But it wasn't the Latin lesson or being told I was
different that I remember most about that first evening. It wasn't the shock of cold air rushing inside my
shell or the terrible task of scrabbling my way out.
It wasn't even that first thrilling sensation when one
moment you're curled tight as a pencil shaving, and
the next you're free as a bird (if you'll pardon the pun),
and the world is closer, louder, at your very wingtips.

No.

What I remember most about that first day is that I
was tired. Even as I listened to the two tiny voices calling for help inside those two other shells, I fell asleep.

And by the time I woke up, one of those voices
was gone.

Fritz Feldman's Official
Medical Logbook
Medical Log, May 6

Today in English, Mrs. Cuthbert said that if I wanted to become a doctor someday, I should start writing like one, and *oh Mylanta*, I thought that was a GREAT idea, so here starts my "Official Medical Log."

- Age: 11 years 10 months
- Weight: 122.3 lbs
- Height: 53 in (if I measured right)
- Current status: 1 ingrown toenail, 2 spider bites, 1 possible heart palpitation, questionable lump

I think that about covers the medical stuff.

I guess I should tell you a little bit about me. There are probably only two really important things you should know.

1. I want to be a medical practitioner when I grow up. (That's a *doctor*, in regular terms.)

My dad's an accountant at a big hospital with all kinds of doctors—brain surgeons, heart doctors. . . . I'm actually not sure what kind of doctor I'll be, but I'm pretty sure it won't be one of those. I don't want to specialize in the emergency stuff either. Or geriatrics (that's medicine for old people). Nothing where you, you know, have to try to save somebody's life?

2. I'm the only almost-twelve-year-old I know who has a job.

I work at Pete's Pet (and Parrot!) Shack every Monday, Wednesday, and Friday after school. It's not *exactly* legal, but Mom said it was okay since she works late and Grandpa isn't there to let me in after I get home from school anymore. She worries I'll get locked out again, like that time the neighbor's dog was sniffing around the rhododendron bush and ate our hidden key. (PS Did you know you can get frostbite in just thirty minutes? It's true. I didn't get frostbite because it wasn't exactly cold, but anything's possible.) At least at the shop Mom knows where I am. And if anyone asks, I tell them Pete's *technically* my childcare technician.

(Pete says not to mention the five bucks he gives me every day.)

It's a good job. I mostly sweep and stock shelves, but sometimes it's exciting. Like when I get to take a sick guinea pig to the back and put him in the Infirmary to get better.

Or when a shipment of twenty-four tarantulas comes in, and I have to show Pete that his handwriting on the order really DOES look like a *24* and not a *2*. That's why I get to fill out all the orders now.

Or like today, when I got to watch a baby African grey parrot hatch. I was the very first person in the whole world to welcome him to earth. That's a big responsibility, I think. I didn't really know what to say, so I just introduced myself, and I kind of gave him a name. And just to keep him company, I told him about his genus and species and the differences between primates and birds (thumbs, for example)— stuff like that.

But later, when I was cleaning out litter boxes

in the back, I noticed one of the other eggs didn't look right. A tiny bird was halfway out of his shell, and he wasn't alive. I didn't touch him at all, but I could see that he hadn't absorbed his yolk sac, and when that's the case, there's just nothing you can do. I looked it up.

Pete wasn't happy. He told me to take the baby bird out and feed it to the snakes. Don't worry—I didn't do it. But I *did* notice the egg incubator was at 97.3 degrees. A whole degree too low! That's a big deal when you're hatching chicks. I fixed it and added water to increase the humidity, so hopefully the last egg will hatch all right.

I'll check on Alastair and the other egg when I go back in on Wednesday and let you know what happens.

Signed: **Dr. Francis Fitzpatrick Feldman, MD** ← (I think this will be my future signature.)

PS I just realized I forgot to bring the dead bird home. I was going to bury him.

PPS I don't know why I'm telling you this, but during lunch today, I found a dollar in the school library's Latin dictionary. I didn't want to be sneaky, so I gave it to Mr. Hall, the librarian, and as I was leaving, this little old lady who was helping him put books on the shelf waved her feather scarf at me and shouted, "Ah! Rara avis! Farewell!" It was kind of weird.

(Note to self: Remember to look up what "rara avis" means.)

Dear Everett,

I bought a feather boa the other day—a
lovely red one. I know you'll think I'm a
birdbrain, but I truly needed it. I wore it to
the post office. I wore it while getting my
hair set. I liked that boa so much I wore it
to church! Betty, Joan—all the girls loved
it. Delores Greenbush thought it was
scandalous, but I told her, "Delores, if the
good Lord made a cardinal, he obviously
had no problem with red feathers."

That shut her up.

Anyhoo, I took my boa to the market
yesterday. I'd just gotten my oatmeal and two
bananas, when somewhere around the canned
peas, that cell phone Henry gave me started
ringing. It was the school, looking for help in
the library for a few hours, so I quick bought
my things and skedaddled on over there.

Well, I'll be darned, it wasn't until my curls hit the pillow later that night that I realized I never bought food for the fish! I didn't bother changing out of my nightdress, just threw on my slicker and boa and headed on down to the pet shop since it's close. Peter was just locking up when I got there, but you know me.

I got my ways.

And there I was, waiting for my fish flakes, when next thing I know, doesn't he come out of the back room, throwing a fine fit over a dead bird! Said he'd told his stock boy to get rid of it earlier. Went on and on about it.

Out of nowhere I said, "Peter, you go on and get me a box, and *I'll* take care of it!"

He did it. He boxed it up.

And I walked out carrying my fish flakes and an expired bird.

Well, I wasn't about to bring the poor thing home where Tiger could get to it. It deserved a proper burial.

A burial at sea was too dramatic. The dumpster behind the building just wasn't kind. I thought about burying it in your flower boxes, but that seemed crowded.

And I couldn't go digging up a spot in the park, on property I don't own! I did all I could think of.

You guessed it. I went to the cemetery.

It was closed when I got there, but I marched myself past those NO TRESPASSING signs and buried it there on the only piece of land I got.

It almost felt right, too, like a cemetery was the proper place for a bird. Who knows if the little twittering ghost of the thing won't be singing over the flowers, building nests in the crooks of the stones, and making friends with all our dearly departed. Animals do have a way of keeping people company, I told myself. And then I had a thought.

What if I planned my own little get-together? You know, with some old folks— and some animals! I could make a flyer. I'll invite the gals! (Not Delores, she's a pest.)

I think that could catch on, don't you?

Oh, would you look at me, I've been rambling away here! I was only meaning to give you an update on Henry. Tried calling when I got home, but he was working late again. I told his machine that if he can spare a minute, he should give his old mother a ring. For all he knows, I've been carted off to jail for trespassing. And you know what they say . . .

There's no end to the mischief an eighty-year-old woman can get into when wearing a red feather boa.

> Love,
> Your glamorous
> criminal of a wife

PS Forgot to mention, while I was volunteering in the school library today, I took the opportunity to hide a few dollars in books, just like I used to do when Henry was little. (It got that little penny-pincher to read, remember?) Well, one very honest young man found one of the bills and turned it in. I thought it was real respectable. A rare thing these days.

I bet he calls his mother all the time.

CHAPTER 2

Pete blows into the back room of the pet shop, makes a beeline for the line of glass cases across the way, and dumps an exceedingly large rabbit into an empty one.

"Babs," grunts the guinea pig next door.

"Porky," answers the rabbit in a throaty voice. "Back here in the Infirmary again? I was hoping you got sold this time."

"Sold? And leave you?" Porky's eyes twinkle mischievously. "You couldn't live without me, Babs."

"I'd manage," she replies coolly.

Behind me, Aggie's voice chirps out from under a towel. "Alastair! You can count to ten now. I've got my hiding spot!" At Aggie's insistence we've played about a hundred games of hide-and-seek over the last few weeks. Being that there are only two places to hide—under towel number one or under towel number two—it's not very challenging. But I oblige.

"All right, Ag. Here goes. One, two . . ."

In the far corner of the room, Pete tears a box off the shelf and begins to untangle the mangled knot of leashes inside when there's a rap on the storeroom door. He looks over his shoulder and frowns. "I may have mentioned this on the phone every day for the last five weeks, Mrs. Plopky," he shouts, "but you can't take the expensive stuff! I'll let you borrow some tarantulas for your little dance party—I'm up to my ears in tarantulas! But nothing else!"

I continue to count. ". . . three, four . . ."

"Now, Peter," says a muffled voice from behind the door. "I'm not looking to give anybody a conniption with your spiders. Lord knows everyone signed up for my Polka with Puppies group is pushing a hundred. No, no, this is supposed to be a nice senior social hour—with animals."

". . . Five . . ."

Pete slaps a hand over his face and groans. "Mrs. Plopky, you're a swell customer, but if I start letting you borrow pets for all your little shindigs, people are going to start coming in here with the same idea. Use one of your own animals! What about that cat I sold you?"

"That cat—" The door bursts open, and the squat shape of an old woman with red feathers around her neck steps inside. She settles a fist on each hip and stares at Pete, who withers a little under her gaze. "That cat is a miser. No, sir. Folks signed up for puppies. I need something cute and cuddly."

"Take the guinea pig," offers Babs, and Porky shoots her a dirty look.

I glance back at the Aggie-shaped lump under towel number two. With all this distraction, I can't remember what number I've left off on.

Pete sighs and grabs another box from the shelf. "You want something to bring with you, something cute, take a parakeet. They're cheap."

Porky nods. "Yeah, take a parakeet. Pigs don't

polka. Barely got knees. Besides"—he coughs, unconvincingly—"think I got a touch of the swine flu."

A regular in the Infirmary, Porky's forever faking an illness for what he calls "a trip to the sauna." An incubator, his own food dish, and a few days away from the kids and customers, and Porky's a new pig—I mean, rodent. This particular trip, however, has been no spa visit. He had a run-in last week with a piece of plastic broccoli some kid threw in his cage. "Thought it tasted a little rubbery," Porky said later.

"Or what about this guy here?" suggests Pete, gesturing to Porky. "See? That sounds fun. Guinea Pig Polka or whatever you're calling it. Or how about"—Pete looks thoughtful—"Jig with Some Guinea Pigs?"

Porky promptly chokes on a pellet. "*Jig with*— JIG? I'll give you a jig with a guinea pig!" He heaves another pellet in Pete's direction. (It misses by twenty feet.)

"Thought you were a gerbil there for a second, McPorkster," Babs says with a smirk. She raises an eyebrow and waits.

Porky takes a long look at her, sniffs, and returns to his food bowl. "I got much more refinement than a gerbil," he growls.

Meanwhile, back in our incubator, Aggie's given up on our game. "Who's that?" she asks, joining me at the glass and nodding at the visitor. She gives a little cough, and I frown. That's the fourth cough today.

"I don't know," I answer slowly. "Never seen another human back here but Pete and that Fritz kid."

Aggie coughs again. "I like her feathers."

Mrs. Plopky wanders past the glass boxes of the Infirmary. "Guinea pigs just don't have that pizzazz," she's saying, tapping a finger against her chin.

"Pigs got pizzazz," Porky mutters from his case.

Mrs. Plopky turns and scans the room a final time, her finger tap-tap-tapping away. All at once, her eyes land—on me. "How about a *parrot?*"

Pete leaps from the box of chew toys he's half inside and smacks his head into the hanging light-bulb, sending it spinning in circles. It knocks his cap off, and the top of Pete's head gleams like a beacon with every swing of the bulb.

I scowl. *Feather picker.*

"NO PARROTS!" shouts Pete. "Parrots are money in the bank! I hate parrots, but parrots pay the bills!"

Aggie gasps.

"He don't mean it, hon," says Babs.

"He means it," says Porky.

"It's okay," I tell Aggie. "Pete just doesn't want to give you up because he loves you so much." (It's wholly untrue, but Aggie's sensitive.)

"Oh." Aggie brightens. "Oh, of course! Pete's so funny like that."

"A real hoot," I say through clenched beak as Pete scrambles to gather his hat from an open box of cat collars. The light continues to sway over his bald patch. I scowl again.

It's quite the nasty trick Pete takes such care of the long, gray feathers that peek out from under his baseball cap. I'd admired them for a while. So did Aggie. Until one day he took that cap off.

Balder than a chick up top.

There's nothing worse than a feather picker.

They tend to be anxious sorts. They lack confidence, self-control, feathers (obviously), and a good amount of brain cells. Familiar with the term "birdbrain"?

Feather picker.

Somebody saw some bird with a few tufts left and two blank eyes goggling in two different directions, looking hungry to pick whatever was left, and thereby determined all birds were idiots. Hence: birdbrain.

We cannot all be judged by the disheveled madness of a few.

Mrs. Plopky plants herself in front of the door, blocking entry to the store, and begins to do a little shimmy. A forgotten pink curler pinned to her head bounces as she tappity-taps in a circle. Even her eyes dance, the wrinkles around them deepening. "Peter, dear," she sings. "If you let me borrow a few puppies for my group, one of my fuddy-duddy friends might decide to purchase one. . . ."

Pete straightens and pulls his cap on. "Fine," he growls. "You win. Grab some puppies and bring 'em back here. I'll put 'em in crates."

"Oh goody!" the old woman exclaims as she runs back into the shop, curler bobbing behind her. She returns a few minutes later with an armful of slobbering Labrador pups. As soon as the door closes, one wriggles from her grasp and then another. "Oh! Oh dear!"

Soon all four puppies are tearing through cartons of dog biscuits and pulling flea powder off shelves. One's eating kitty litter, another leaves a warm puddle next to a sack of cedar shavings.

The room's a riot of barking and Pete's cursing, but at last the puppies are wrangled up and locked in carriers.

"Go on and put them in my car, Peter," says Mrs. Plopky, straightening the feathers around her neck. She reaches up and pinches Pete's cheek. "I'll have them back by Tuesday. And don't you worry! I'll tell all my friends about you!"

Pete grunts, clearly annoyed he's been duped into the whole business, but obeys.

"And I'll make you a pie! I'm a very fine pie baker!" she shouts after him. She tucks her pocketbook in the crook of her arm and, turning to leave, spots our case again, stops, and peers inside. I hide myself under a loose corner of towel, while Aggie flaps her wings and garbles a greeting.

"Well, would you look at that?" she says to Aggie. "Aren't you a little darling?" She turns her sights on me then, and I try my best to melt into the corner. "And you—"

Behind a pair of thick glasses, the watery blue of her eyes bores into me.

"You," she says again. "You're no darling, are you?" The corners of her mouth curl.

I swallow. I'm not sure I appreciated that comment.

Even if it is true.

"Cat got your tongue?" Mrs. Plopky asks.

As if I'd ever let that happen.

In a flash of pink skin and spiny feathers, I rush the glass, squawk, and snap my beak, thinking it should scare her off.

She doesn't seem to notice. "That's what I

thought. You're no darling, but you're feisty. I like feisty," she says, then points at my feet. "Don't look now, but you stepped in a little something."

She trots out into the shop, and the door swings on its hinges and comes to a groaning stop. I look down at my feet.

A little something.

Well.

That's a nice way of putting it.

CHAPTER 3

"When do you think we'll eat?" Aggie asks.

I crane my neck to get a peek at the space under the door, and sure enough, the thread of light's been snuffed out. I put on a brave face. "Pretty soon, I think," I answer.

Aggie flaps her wings and grins. "Oh good, because I'm starving."

The barks, squawks, squeaks, and purrs in the pet shop quieted long ago. Somewhere on the sales floor, crickets chirp faintly from inside those $3.99 Styrofoam containers they get themselves stuck inside. A hamster falls out of the wheel he's been sleeping in. Here and there the snore of a turtle drifts through the dark.

Across from us, Porky's fallen asleep in his food dish, mouth agape. A string of drool gleams in the dismal light of the exit sign.

All right, so I lied about the "pretty soon" part. Crickets, snoring, drooling in the dark—you add it all up and it means only one thing:

Ol' Pete will not be returning to feed us.

It isn't the first time. Not the first time I've thought about taking a nice bite out of him either. Pete says he hates parrots? The feeling's mutual.

"I bet Pete's just feeding the puppies first this time, huh," Aggie says, shaking her head sadly. "Poor Mama Pete, so many mouths to feed. We'll just be patient. Right, Alastair?"

I smile at her and feel a little of my anger fall away.

If anyone *is* a different species, it's my sister. Aggie.

She came into the world, in a warm beam of incubator sun, a full three days after my own entry. Aggie's first words to me? *Oh,* there *you are!* As if she were the one waiting on me and not the other way around.

I'd tapped hellos, coaxed, *willed* her here. And after I helped her chip away at her shell, she arrived like a tiny sunrise and with so much light, I never did ask if she'd heard the voice inside the other egg. The one that never hatched, just disappeared. I didn't want to ruin it, didn't want to make her sad. Sadness has claws, I've found. And keeping them from my sister is all I've ever wanted for her since.

Above us, the heat lamp pops and flickers out. Aggie gives a startled wail.

A stab of cold air blows in from the air-conditioning vent in the corner, and Aggie shivers beside me. I grab the edge of the towel with my beak, do my best to wrap it around us, and hold my breath, waiting to see what the lamp will do. A night without heat is certain death for a pair of hatchlings.

Aggie pats me with a thorny wing, and her beak chatters. "Don't worry, Alastair. Pete won't let us down."

Out of the quiet depths of the pet shop, the rabbits cackle. A puppy yelps and goes silent. Something hoots in the distance, and Aggie cocks her head, listening. My ears prick too at the sound of one of Aggie's coughs.

Another. I've lost count today.

A few fiddle-playing crickets play a mournful dirge. A funeral march.

We'll see about that.

I stalk to the edge of the glass and rap my beak against it. Nothing happens.

I rap harder. This time the lamp above us flickers, sparks, and blazes back to life.

"There. Light's back on," I say, stalking back to our nest. "Don't worry, Ag. *I'll* take care of you." And I will. I may have slept on the job once, but not again. There's a reason Aggie stays warm and fed and far from sorrow's grip. There's a reason she hatched all right.

I made sure of it.

I will always make sure of it.

Aggie bobs her head and smiles. "You and Mama Pete—you never let me down," she says, and I'm about to tell her that statement is only half-true, when her forehead wrinkles, and she clears her throat. "Um,

Alastair? Do you think if Pete feeds the puppies first, then maybe the kittens will be next, and then us?"

I sigh. I'm not fond of lying to her, but it's better this way. "That's probably about right," I answer. "Puppies first, then the kittens. Should be any minute now."

"Oh, but what about the gerbils? They need to eat."

"Right. The gerbils—"

A head pops up across the way in the Infirmary. A bandaged head with bandaged eyes and half a tail. Aggie lowers her voice to a whisper. "I know you don't think much of them, but they're not so bad. They're just troubled!"

"They're barbarians, Aggie."

She looks over at the gerbil, who's now sniffing around blindly and talking to himself, a bit of spittle gathering at the corner of his mouth. Aggie winces. "They're good at heart, though—just yesterday that one asked me if I wanted a knuckle sandwich!"

I rest my case.

See, I've learned a few things very early in my young parrot life. I'll give you the basics.

One: You come into this world very cold and very naked. Your only job is to grow an armor of feathers and survive.

And two: Trust no one. Not even your mother. It's a gerbil-eat-gerbil world, everyone clawing for a spot at the top of the food chain. A bird can't get caught with his feathers pulled over his eyes.

He'd better be sharpening his talons.

"How about I tell you a bedtime story while we wait?" I suggest.

Aggie sniffles and squeezes in closer. "Okay."

The sharp spines of her new feathers poke into my side, and she closes her eyes and smiles in that perfect Aggie way: a little lopsided, but sort of precious, you know?

"Tell the one about the stars," she says.

"It's like someone took a handful of light, threw it up in the air, and it broke apart in a million tiny sparks."

"And the sky?"

"The sky's blue—*periwinkle-powder-bright*, to be exact."

"Ooh, I like that color," Aggie says.

I tell Aggie about things I've never seen, places I've never been. I know them, though, somewhere deep in my bones. Like some kind of instinct.

Like some long-ago bird whispered stars to my heart, made clouds scuttle through my veins. I know trees: pine and palm, the kola nut and the wandering mangrove. I'm sure of things called flocks and family, and that good, foraging, attentive mothers *have* to exist.

I know what it is to fly.

"The sky is a brilliant blue," I tell Aggie. "And the bluer it gets, the closer you are."

"To where?" Aggie asks.

"To home."

If there's another thing I know, it's that there's a place called home. Some nest high in a tree, where you can watch clouds and count stars. A place with no Petes. A place where they don't forget to feed you. A place where I'll never have to listen to Aggie's belly growl again.

Whatever it takes, I'm going to find that home for me and Aggie. I will.

Like most things, it takes more than a dream and a couple of thumbs to get what you want. It takes determination, strength.

It's not just wings you need to fly.

Pete barrels into the storeroom the next morning, half-moons of sweat staining the space under his arms. "Sorry 'bout that!" he says briskly. "Had to pick up my takeout at Tasty Panda before it closed last night! Didn't want my wontons getting cold!"

"Yeah. Hate it when my wontons get cold," I hear Porky grunt from his darkened case opposite us.

Pete flips on the light.

"Hey!" Porky yells. (By the way, if you thought most guinea pigs had high, squealy voices, you'd be wrong. Porky sounds like he's swallowed a bucket or two of the gravel Pete keeps in the back for the fish tanks.) "Can a pig get some fresh lettuce or something over here? Cripes! Thought this place was supposed to be the spa!"

From out of the corner of my eye, I see him turn to me and hold up a slimy piece of green between two tiny claws. "Must be a *health* spa, right, fella? Yech." He flings the lettuce aside, where it slaps on the incubator window and sticks. "You waiting on breakfast too?"

"Late-night snack, actually," I answer.

"Eh, sorry, kid. I can share some pellets if you like. They taste like cedar shavings, but they work in a pinch."

"Thanks, but no."

"It's coming, it's coming," grumbles Pete, grabbing water, food, and the little plastic tubes that spit meals into our gullets. "Dang birds better be worth all the trouble. Ol' Pete could use a few thousand to tide him over until the Christmas rush," he mutters. "Got other things to do 'sides feed *birds* all day."

"What about guinea pigs?" shouts Porky. "I'm gonna turn into a pellet over here if I don't get some greens!"

Aggie, still asleep, lets out a whimper. I nudge her awake.

"Is the story over?" she asks with a yawn. Even with a full night's sleep, her head droops. She looks like a stuffed cat toy that's lost a bit too much of its stuffing. Being careful not to catch a claw in the terry cloth, she stumbles trying to inch out of the corner we slept in. I offer her my wing, and she leans on it heavily. "Oh, I *am* hungry," she whispers.

"I know you are, Ag. Don't worry—Pete's here," I say, first guiding her, then pushing her to the middle of our glass box, where Pete will see her straightaway. Back in the corner, I hide myself under a towel. If Pete runs out of food, as he's done twice already this week, he'll run out of my breakfast instead of hers.

And I can handle it.

"Here we go, little moneybags," I hear Pete say. "Not sure which one you are, but eat up!"

With each of Aggie's gulps, I swallow a sigh of relief. When it's my turn to eat, I keep one eye on the food bowl and one on Pete's hand.

"You sure eat a lot," says Pete. "You'd think I needed to whip up a whole extra bowl! Geez, I feel like that Tortelloni lady from TV."

Pete says this every time he feeds us. You'd think he'd whip up that extra bowl already. He never does.

The bowl of mush gets low, and Pete's patience gives out.

Mine gave out overnight.

While I fed Aggie stories into the wee hours of morning, I fed myself with thoughts of revenge.

I can see I've timed my plan just right.

Pete tips the plastic tube toward my mouth, and I wait for what he's about to say next. . . .

"If you two weren't worth so much, I'd probably feed you to the snakes."

It's then that I bite.

And strangely enough, though I haven't learned to fly yet . . .

I find myself soaring—no—*hurtling* through the air.

CHAPTER 4

I did not become snake bait.

I did, however, get myself pitched against the wall like a limp piece of lettuce.

"He's waking up! He's waking up!"

Pete doesn't let him hang around our box often, but I'd know this chirp anywhere. Fritz reaches down to grab me. "Come here, little fella," he says.

A single finger brushes against me, and a fire ignites in my left wing and burns through my shoulder. My stomach lurches. I look over to see pinned to my side the bandaged mummy of my wing, heavy—and dead.

"Poor little guy," says Fritz, slowly lifting me

from the glass box and setting me in a nest of towels on the desk. His forehead creases, and a pink tongue peeks out of the side of his mouth. "Don't worry. I've done this before. I was sitting in Grandpa's old food truck in the backyard once, and a robin crashed right into the window."

"Alastair!"

Aggie. She flutters her wings and bobs her head beside me, eyes bright with excitement. "Oh, Alastair! I was so worried! When Pete threw you against that wall, I thought—well, I don't even want to say it. But you're well! You're awake, anyway. I'm so relieved. But Fritz says you've broken your wing—" Her face crumples into a look of utter despair. "How terrible—a bird with a broken wing."

Great. I've become a cliché.

"It's okay, though," Aggie adds quickly. "You're not *broken* broken, not like ruined or anything—not wrecked . . . oh dear." She looks flustered. "Only—only—"

I force a smile. "*Ruined*, huh?"

Aggie blushes, and the corners of her beak curl

into her trademark smile. "Fritz fixed it," she says softly, then fills me in on everything that's happened while I've been "out" (a careless lack of consciousness I'll be sure to avoid in the future). After Pete nearly killed me, he was sorry, she tells me. Said something like *If this here bird doesn't shake a leg, my wallet's gonna turn to dust.* Aggie thought that sounded very touching.

"And you wouldn't believe it, Alastair—it's the first day of summer vacation, and Fritz came in early, and he was able to fix your wing, and Pete said he could work extra to take care of us so Pete doesn't throw any more birds." Aggie says this is very lucky on our part. Fritz has informed her that he will only be absent when Pete gets sick of him and kicks him out, but because we need so many meals, we can rightly assume Fritz will rarely leave our sides. Aggie's grin's as wide as a guinea pig's gut. "Isn't that great?"

"That's great, Aggie."

"He's very happy to help, you know. Normally, he's only got his newt Charles to take care of, and raising us is good practice anyway—for his career. You're going to love him—I just know it!" Aggie barely breathes between sentences. "He loves the Fourth of July and cheese curls. And he absolutely loves bologna sandwiches dipped in grape jelly. They're his favorite because he says they taste like a Swedish meatball. I think I'd like a Swedish meatball. It sounds so fancy."

Across the room, Fritz bangs and chops and mixes mush. "Just getting your dinner ready," he calls over his shoulder. "You two are gonna love this. Your first taste of real food!"

"Oh, yeah," says Aggie. "Also, he has a magic glowing box."

"A what?" I ask.

"That glowing box—behind you."

I turn my head to see a box on the edge of the desk. It indeed glows.

"It's very magical," Aggie says in a serious whisper. "Fritz sat there a lot, looking into it. I think it must tell him things, because every so often he points at it and tells me something new. That's what happened when he said your wing would heal in two to four weeks. Two to four weeks! Isn't that great news? And did you know we can learn to talk—like humans, I mean?"

Sure I know.

Fritz serves us our dinner. "There's some peppers there and zucchini. I had some cherries in my lunch. I put those in too," he says before going back to his seat at the glowing box.

I'm instantly very grateful there's more to life than mush.

With her mouth stuffed with food, Aggie tells me the box has said we should've been eating vegetables by now (fine), and fruits (I've already decided my diet should consist of cherries and ONLY cherries). In addition, we are extremely intelligent (clearly), and we can live up to sixty years (excellent news).

However . . .

The glowing box has told Fritz that African greys can be vain, suspicious, and opinionated; greys can have irrational phobias; we hold grudges; and when raised apart from our bird parents, we tend to think of ourselves as human instead of embracing our identity as birds.

"It's part of our biology," Aggie says plainly. "It's science."

I'd say it's pretty clear we can't trust this thing.

Finally Fritz pushes back his chair, stands, and stretches. "I think that computer screen burned my retinas to a crisp," he says, rubbing his eyes. He carries us back to our glass box across the room. "It's almost closing time. I've got to get you two settled. Stay here a second—I'll be right back."

Aggie yawns. "It was a long day, wasn't it, Alastair?" she asks.

Long isn't quite the word for it. I thought it was bad starting out the day hungry. Now I'm damaged. It's embarrassing, frankly. What's a guy without the use of his wing?

Plus, the thing's throbbing like a cricket fiddle.

Aggie falls asleep quickly, but while shut-eye should come easy with a full belly, my wing seems to think otherwise. I watch as Fritz grabs an empty aquarium and takes it into the shop. He comes back for a few handfuls of cedar shavings, a food bowl, a towel, and an array of brightly colored toys. "That should do it," he says to himself. "Next up: dinner for the other patients in the Infirmary."

Fritz distributes food bowls—one to Babs, one to an ancient tortoise with a cracked shell, and another he tosses into the gerbil case and quickly slams the top shut. He stops at Porky's case. "Hey, Porky. I thought you were feeling better, but you don't look so good." He places a dish next to him. "Better stay in the Infirmary another night."

Soon as Fritz moves on, Porky grins his two yellow teeth at me and winks. "Don't be alarmed, kid," he whispers. "Zucchini calls for another night at the spa."

Beside me, Aggie sighs contentedly in her sleep, and I give her a reassuring pat and smooth a few feathers that are out of place. One at the top of her head springs back, and I gently push it down again. And again.

Fritz snaps off the glowing box and grabs his bag from the desk chair. "I think that's it. I'll be back bright and early, okay, guys?" He makes his way toward us, then reaches in and plucks Aggie from our box. "Good night, Alastair. Say good-bye to your sister."

Wait—

I freeze. By the time I realize he's stealing Aggie, I make a hasty attempt to bite Fritz's hand off, but my beak catches air.

And then . . .

She's gone. Just like that, Aggie's gone.

The door to the back room swings closed behind them, and I'm left staring into the beady eyes of the gerbil pressed up against the glass across the way. He'd perked up at the prospect of blood. He scowls and stalks back to his food dish.

Pain races through my wing and into my chest.

"Hey there, fella," Porky says softly. "It'll be okay. Fritz there—he's a good kid. Wherever he took Aggie, she'll be all right." He puts up two of four fingers. "Pig's honor."

"Yeah, hon," Babs pipes up. "She's probably just out there in the shop. The rabbits will look after her. They're used to a few extra kids. Gloria's looking after sixteen of mine right now."

Porky agrees. "Sure, sure! And then there's my missus! Honey of a pig, she is! Loves throwing welcome parties. She's pretty good with scared birds."

"Stop." I spit the word out. The pain, the talking, it's suddenly too much. Everything's wrong. Even my feathers feel out of place, and I feel an immediate urge to fix them. "I'm—I'm trying to hear Aggie."

"Oh. Yeah. Sure," says Porky.

The three of us strain to listen for any sign of my sister beyond the door.

Squeak. Squeak. Squeak. Squeak.

"Hamster wheel," notes Porky.

There's a series of crashes and scratches and bloodcurdling screams.

"Gerbils," adds Babs.

Something rumbles low and loud. "Sorry," says Porky, looking sheepish. "My stomach knows there's zucchini around."

I try calling out to Aggie to see if she answers, but the effort stokes the fire in my wing, and I have to sit in silence as the pain subsides.

Interesting thing, though.

As that fire in my wing cools to embers, thoughts of escape come blazing to life.

Medical Log, June 17

- Age: 11 years 11 months
- Weight: 121.8 lbs
- Height: 53 in
- Current status: 1 ingrown toenail, elevated heart rate, clammy palms, pimple-or possible tumor???

I have news. I have two birds!

Rara avis. Or *rarae aves*, I guess I should say. *Rare birds.* The African greys I was telling you about!

They're not exactly mine. Pete's selling them in the shop—or he *will* be once they're old enough, and once Alastair gets better. Pete accidentally broke Alastair's wing today. But I think I fixed it. I made a nice sling and thought Pete would be impressed, but all he said was to keep Alastair in the back for the next couple of weeks. He doesn't want customers thinking he's selling damaged goods.

Here's the great part, though. Pete says from now on, Alastair and Aggie are my responsibility. It's up to me to raise them. I get to come to the store three times a day for feedings, which isn't a problem now that school's out and Mom's agreed I don't have to go to basketball camp again. (When I told her that last year Ryan and Tanner Bigler made *me* the ball at camp, she was pretty okay with it.)

I'm finding out parrots are a lot of work. Some of the stuff I read even said they can be as smart and needy as human toddlers, and I believe it. I've had to do a bunch of research on how to hold them and get them to trust me, how to make their food and give them showers and clip their wings so they can't fly away, and how to give them enough attention and everything so they behave. And like I said, Alastair's wing is broken, so I have to keep an eye on that.

Oh, and he has a biting problem.

I guess birds that bite (Alastair, for example) like

to be in control. Or they're bored or scared. It's not his fault. Parrots who never know their parents can have all sorts of problems. I read that, too. It really makes you think.

I've only seen Dad once in the past two years—last summer when Fiona and I flew out to California for a month. (I probably forgot to tell you my dad doesn't live with us. He and my mom got divorced when I was three.) It was a really great trip, though. Dad even took me to the hospital once, so I could see his office. I got to see a real live operating room too! But I miss him a lot. So I bet it's really hard never meeting or being with either one of your parents.

I'm not sure if I can help Alastair's biting, but I'm going to try. And I'm definitely going to try to get Aggie healthier. I'm going to watch for things like allergies or infections or changes in their eating or behavior. I even need to track their poop, which is gross, but it tells you a lot. I thought about making a medical chart like the one I made for Grandpa.

But then I thought it probably wasn't a good idea.

Signed: **Dr. Francis Fitzpatrick Feldman, MD** ← maybe this one's better

PS I should have told you more about Aggie! She's so, so sweet. She sat with me and listened to everything I said. I think she's already attached to me. My research said that could happen.

But it didn't tell me that I'd be so attached to her already too.

CHAPTER 5

"You just made me remember a joke, Alastair!" Aggie's giggling already. "Tell me if you've heard this one. The puppies told it to me, and it's *hilarious.*"

So, Porky and Babs were right. My sister's living roughly twenty feet away at the front of the store. It might as well be a mile except for the three times a day her captor brings her to the back room so he can feed us and let us walk around to get some exercise. Aggie thinks this means I should forgive Fritz.

I wholeheartedly disagree.

"Aggie, you were telling me about the lock on the shop's door, remember?" We're perched on the desk.

Distracted, Aggie's on tiptoe, trying to see what Fritz is doing over by the small refrigerator wedged into the corner. ". . . About how I could probably twist it with my beak and we could sneak out that way?" I continue hopefully.

She turns to look at me. "Yeah, but then I remembered this joke."

I sigh. "Fine. What's your joke?"

"Okay, here goes. Which animal in the pet shop has more lives than a cat?" Aggie claps a wing over her beak to keep the answer from bubbling out.

"I don't know, Ag. Which one?"

"A frog!" she shouts. "Get it?"

She hasn't quite figured out how to *deliver* a good joke, so I help her out. "A frog, why?"

"Oh, yeah! Because frogs *croak* all the time! Get it? Frogs croak. Cats die, but they have nine lives. Do you get it, Alastair?"

"I get it."

"Gosh, I thought that was a good one! When you were talking about escaping again, it made me think of it."

"I'm not sure why," I answer.

"Well, because we can't fly . . ."

I cringe.

"You especially, Alastair. Your wing still hurts, remember?"

"A minor detail," I grumble, feeling the color bloom in my cheeks as I try to pretend what she said doesn't bother me.

"Yeah . . ." Aggie waddles over to a set of plastic cups Fritz has given her to play with and begins tossing them off the desk. "But whenever you talk about escaping, it makes me think of, you know—death."

Fabulous.

It's a quiet summer afternoon a few weeks into my "rehabilitation," as Fritz calls it. Except, the wing still hurts, and my chest hasn't felt much better. Somewhere around the heart area there's a twinge that kicks in every time Fritz scoots Aggie off to her new case behind the front register. And this conversation? It's doing a real number on it.

Must have a pellet stuck in there somewhere.

Across the room, Fritz, who's been chopping

vegetables all the while, piles the last chunks of potato into our bowls. "Wait till you guys see what I got," he says as he snatches us up and settles our picnic on the worn floorboards next to him.

I immediately stalk to a dark corner under the desk, a piece of property I've lately claimed whenever Fritz lets me out. I get a good amount of sulking done under there. I expect Aggie to follow like she usually does, but she toddles closer to Fritz and digs in to her food bowl. The pellet in my chest digs in deeper.

"You should've seen all the neat stuff they had there! There were cages bigger than this room and a million toys!" Fritz chatters, unloading his backpack into a large heap in the middle of the floor. He'd scurried into the room earlier, pack stuffed and spilling its colorful papers and pamphlets like a rainbow behind him. Reminded me of last week's visitor in the Infirmary, actually.

Some kid fed crayons to one of the puppies.

"And I got to meet a whole bunch of parrots that actually talk. One's name was Charlie Brown, and he kept saying 'Good grief! Good grief!' It was awesome. Oh, that reminds me . . ." Fritz drops a handful of pages, skips over to the shelves, and selects a cricket from a Styrofoam container. He lifts the lid on a small aquarium in the Infirmary and drops the cricket inside, where a fat newt sits awkwardly on a fake rock. The newt left his tail behind yesterday when a customer tried to grab him.

"Eat up, newt," says Fritz. "My newt Charles lost his tail once. You'll need to eat well if you want to regrow it."

I watch as the creature stalks his prey, captures it, and gobbles it down. I look over to see if Aggie is as repulsed as I am, but far from being horrified, she seems quite at peace about it.

As if it's *normal* for humans and newts to go around murdering insects.

"Yech," I hear Porky say. "I'll take a pellet any day."

"De-licious," says Fritz, taking his place on the floor again. "You know what they say, right, Aggie? *A cricket a day keeps the doctor away!*"

Aggie answers him with a bob of her head and a squawk and totters over, climbs up his pant leg and shirt, and settles herself in the space beneath his chin. I watch as Fritz cups one hand around her body and rubs his cheek against her spotty feathers. "Good bird, Aggie. You're a good bird, you are."

Aggie closes her eyes and tucks in closer as I cough and try to dislodge this increasingly uncomfortable pellet in my chest.

What's the saying? Sly as a fox? Slippery as a serpent? Fritz is both of those. Slimy as a slug, too.

I make it a point to lecture Aggie later on the unpredictable nature of the human hand and glare at Fritz.

He selects three pamphlets from the top of the pile. "Look at this one: *How to Get Your Grey to Talk in Thirty Days*. Or how about this one: *Parrot Power: Understanding the Grey Way*? Ooh, *African Greys: The Final Frontier*." He sets Aggie down on the floor, slips a hand under the mess of papers, and roots around for a second. "Wait, look at this!"

Fritz proceeds to unroll a large piece of paper and tack it to an empty space on the wall. "It's a poster," he explains. "I got one for home, too."

"Bet you a back scratch it's dumb," I call over to Aggie.

"Shhh," she replies. "Just look."

Fritz finishes taping and steps back to reveal a picture of a small boy with skin the color of a pecan shell, sitting high . . . in a *tree*.

I find myself creeping out from under the desk to get a closer look.

It *is*. It's a tree. A kola nut. I know it in my bones.

Off in the distance, a cluster of straw homes squat in the dirt, the smoke of their fires snaking its way into . . . a *sky*, dotted . . . with *clouds*. I pin my eyes on the blue of it and swallow hard.

The bluer it gets, the closer you are to home.

"Isn't it beautiful?" whispers Aggie. "And that sky's just like I told you, Alastair—just like the sky outside the shop's windows."

"It can't be," I answer. "That's—that's a bluer sky." I swallow again, but the lump in my throat remains a stone.

"Well, I thought it looked the same," Aggie mumbles.

I take another step closer. That sky. It's every-thing I've wanted, everything Aggie and I need. I memorize the color, feel it begin to thump into my veins like a drumbeat.

"I like that boy in the picture," Aggie says. "He reminds me of Fritz." The boy in the poster dangles in the tree, wearing little more than the large cowboy hat tipped on his head and a broad smile. Next to the boy perches a bird like Aggie and me, only the bird's wearing a miniature red bandanna around her neck. The way the bird opens her beak just so makes it look as if she's smiling too.

Along the bottom of the poster Fritz reads, "*Amicus verus est rara avis,*" and steps back to survey the addition to the dreary walls. "I'll figure out what the rest of it means, but as soon as I saw the 'rara avis,' I knew I had to buy it." He feels around in the pile and this time produces a red bandanna printed with feathers. "Well, that and it looks like Aggie sitting there in that tree. Grandp—I mean *Fiona's* gonna like it, I think. Mom, too."

He ties the bandanna around his neck. "I wonder

if Fiona's got a cowboy hat I can borrow," he says to himself as he steps back to show us his getup against the poster. "Like it?"

Not exactly.

Up on his hind legs and pressed against the glass, Porky shakes his head. "I don't know what it is with humans and costumes."

He gestures to the calendar taped to the wall and curling at the edges. It features twelve potbellied pigs in motley attire. There's a pirate pig, a pumpkin pig, a pig dressed like a pilgrim. "My ancestors there," Porky says. "I'm just glad my great-granddaddy Bacon McPorkster didn't see those pictures before he died."

Hmm. Seems to me Porky's a little confused about his ancestry. He's a *guinea* pig.

"C'mere, *partner*," Fritz says, picking up Aggie and putting her on his shoulder.

She takes a few of his feathers in her beak and tugs gently. Fritz smiles. "Hey, silly, quit eating my hair!"

Hair? I thought those were feathers.

Doesn't matter. I'm still part human.

And Pete's still a feather picker.

They stand in front of the poster, facing me. "What do you think, Alastair? It's us, right? Me and Aggie?"

Aggie flaps her wings and squawks her approval.

"Hey, yeah!" agrees Porky. "It's them!"

I'm fairly certain the bottom of my beak is somewhere around my knees.

Fritz sets Aggie on the floor next to me. "It's beautiful, isn't it?" Aggie asks, unable to tear her eyes away from the poster. "It looks just like me and Fritz!"

My feathers itch. A sky like that right in front of us and all Aggie can think of is Fritz.

Fritz. Making our sky, making *everything* about him. I shake my head. "Beautiful, my foot," I say, and stalk to the pile and snatch one of Fritz's papers. One end firmly grasped in my foot, I pull the other end with my beak and begin to shred it into long, jagged strips.

"Hey, stop that," says Fritz. He swats me away and scoots the rest of his loot out of reach. He neglects to take the pamphlet I've stolen. I destroy it until there isn't a readable word left on the page.

But a funny thing happens.

As the paper, the paragraphs, the words, and the punctuation marks go rolling over my tongue, they take on flavor. It's different from the mush Pete piped into our beaks. Different, even, from the array of fruits and vegetables Fritz has been feeding us. It tastes like, like . . .

Information. Like ideas. It tastes, not exactly pleasurable, but satisfying in a different way.

"Here," says Fritz, digging into the bottom of his pack again. "You like paper? I've got some old homework here. I can bring you more from the recycling bin at home. Believe me, you'd be doing me a favor. I never wanna see this stuff again."

He carries over a handful of crumpled papers filled with scratchy handwriting and erasure marks. "Have that," he says, dumping it in front of me and yanking his hand away from my beak. "It's a story I wrote for English. Probably tastes like garbage, though—I got a C-minus on it."

I shred them as I did the brochure, one eye on

Fritz the whole time. Aggie trots over and dips her beak in as well. "This is fun," she says.

"Don't you taste it?" I ask.

"Taste what?"

"I don't know . . . *it*."

"Tastes like paper," says Aggie.

I shake my head. "No, it's not paper. I don't know, it tastes—sour. With something sweet mixed in. It's—" I smack my beak. "It's almost refreshing."

"Nope," mumbles Aggie, with a mouthful. "Just tastes like paper."

But there *is* something. I'm not imagining it. Fritz's garbage tastes . . . fruity . . . *lemony*.

"I don't know why I got a C-minus on it," says Fritz, wiping his nose with his sleeve. "I thought a story about a sour old lemon who gets squashed by a bus and makes some nice refreshing lemonade out of himself was creative. Mrs. Cuthbert said it was disturbing."

Sour? Refreshing? *Lemon?*

I don't know if the story's disturbing, but I do know one thing:

The *taste* of it certainly is.

Dear Everett,

First things first: I'm renaming my senior social club.

A Get-Together with Guinea Pigs, I'm calling it. It's got a real calming feel to it, I think. Old folks don't want puppies; they want calm. It's not about the pizzazz anyway. It's about old gals like me who don't have a place to be on a Friday afternoon.

And speaking of old gals . . .

Irma sent me a brochure today. There was no return address, but I knew it was her. No one else I know buys stamps with kittens on them.

I looked it through, and the Pines seems reasonable. But we already knew it was a perfectly respectable place, didn't we? Driven through it a million times! I liked all the pictures, though. That swimming pool does seem mighty fine. And I've always thought the trees there are just lovely.

I was feeling nearly suckered into it when that one picture got me. The one on the back with that laughing elderly couple? Stopped me in my tracks.

Remember how I used to say we might like to live in a place like that one day? I said you could hole up in the library while I learned to shuffleboard. I promised to attend your two-person book club so long as you agreed to take ballroom dance classes with me, remember? I always thought you'd love being near so many nice folks, even if being social was never your cup of tea.

You old coot. You might've made a friend in Irma's Jack, you know. I hear he reads poetry.

As if it matters. You won't go with me, and I can't bear the thought of going it alone.

Not to mention, who wants to live next to Delores Greenbush, I'd like to know! Not if I can help it!

Did I tell you she showed up at the Shirley River Community Center for my Polka with Puppies group? (Should've put a note on the flyer: *Residents of Apartment #15, Prickly*

Pines need not apply.) I was all excited I had four folks sign up, and then *she* dropped in. The snoop. Came and took notes, she did. Delores's son told Henry all about it. Said I bit off more than I could chew with them pups!

She just had her britches in a bunch over the fact that one whizzed on her loafers.

The Prickly Pines Retirement Village can keep her, I say.

> Love you a whole big batch,
> Bertie

CHAPTER 6

The wing is still a bit of a problem, I'll be honest. Even so, I'm pretty sure Fritz kept me in his infirmary for "observation" a week longer than necessary. But the day's finally come.

Moving day.

If I were the singing type, I might've joined the canaries for a few bars this morning—I was the first bird up.

But it's noon now.

I haven't left this spot under the coatrack since Fritz took off my bandage at eight.

Fritz has invited his sister, Fiona, to the shop this morning to meet me and Aggie before my trek to the sales floor. Predictably, he's spent the last half hour at the glowing box, telling her about gut bacteria.

"Did you know you have two pounds of micro-flora living in your gut, Fiona?" he asks her, never taking his eyes off his reading.

I've learned everything I never needed to know about gut bacteria these last few weeks. Even ate half a library book on it. And that's not all. In the past month, I've eaten a stack of tax forms, three paychecks, a phone book, 124 old math work-sheets, six of Fritz's stories, and one birthday card from Grandma Feldman. (I do not recommend eat-ing birthday cards. There's a sickly-sweet, imitation maple syrup flavor to them that's hard to get past.) I also ate Fritz's bird poster when he wasn't looking. It was terrible.

I hate to admit it, but my favorites have been Fritz's stories. There was a good one about a girl who wears cherry lip balm, and as I haven't eaten any cherries in weeks, it's holding me over, but barely. Then there was another one about Fritz helping an old man who runs a food truck at the fair. The flavor was strong, but sort of depressed, like Pete's day-old French fries or melted ice cream. Gave me indigestion.

Fiona, it appears, doesn't have a taste for gut bacteria either. "I'm thinking of incorporating animals into some of my choreography," she says airily, tapping on one of the glass cases in the Infirmary. "I saw a flyer at the Thrift Mart for this thing with puppies and polka. Animals are probably the next big thing in dance—you know, like goat yoga."

"*Goat* yoga?" says an incredulous Porky, who's back for another spa visit. (He heard the lettuce back here was crisper this week.) He mutters to himself as he picks through his food dish. "Think I'd eat my own leg if somebody dragged me to something like that."

Fiona taps the case for the hundredth time. The gerbil inside is foaming at the mouth. "Dancing and animals—might make for a good senior thesis. What do you think, Fritzerola?"

Fritz barely blinks as he looks deep into the glowing box. "Mm-hmm."

"I imagine *rabbits* are pretty graceful," Fiona says

as she sweeps over to another case, this one brimming with baby bunnies. She reaches in to grab one. "Remember that story Grandpa used to tell us? The one about the rabbit that bit him on the shin while he was cashing a check at the bank? A rabbit! With rabies! In the bank! He always did have terrible luck with animals."

Fritz frowns and looks up. "Wait, what were you saying?"

"Oh, nothing," Fiona replies. "Just thinking about buying one of these rabbits here."

"Hm." Fritz flips off the glowing box. "Didn't you say you had some books for me?" he asks, changing the subject.

Fiona drops the startled bunny back in its case, sprints from the room, and returns a minute later towing a large plastic tub. "I've got a few more in the garage," she says.

"What is this stuff?" Fritz asks, as Fiona snatches a crumpled Burger Den wrapper off the top of the bin and shoots it in the direction of the wastebasket. It hits the wall, lands in an Infirmary fish tank, and sinks slowly to the bottom, where a painted turtle eyes it warily.

"Mostly college textbooks," Fiona answers. "I don't have time to deal with it, with all the extra dance classes I'm taking this summer. Do whatever you want with them."

Fritz lifts a large, bristly, blanketlike thing to eye level.

"My twist-tie quilt," Fiona says matter-of-factly.

Fritz's eyebrows pop up. "Um, great! Thanks?"

"You're welcome," Fiona answers, patting his head and giving him a quick peck on the cheek. She says her good-bye.

"See you," says Fritz.

"Oh!" Fiona turns at the door. "I forgot to tell you. Dad got your message and said he'd try calling again, but he's flying out for a conference in China and, well, the time difference and all. He said he'll call next week."

"Wait, you talked to Dad? Today?" The look of surprise on Fritz's face melts into a frown. "I mean— right. Okay."

Fiona leaves, and Fritz is quiet as he begins to sweep up the storeroom.

"My friend James says that he sells his older brother's textbooks online and makes a fortune," he says finally. "And we're not even stealing them like he does." He props the broom against a stack of pet carriers, drops into his chair, and wheels over to the desk. The glowing box flares to life, and Fritz looks over at Aggie. "What do you think, girl? Think we'll make some money?"

"Oh, yes! Yes, yes, yes!" shouts Aggie, climbing down a shelf and dragging a bowl over to where I've been displaced in the coatrack corner.

"What's he going to buy?" I ask her. "Another dumb bird poster?"

Aggie looks up from her bowl of mango and frowns. "Not nice," she scolds. But she wonders too and squawks as if Fritz could possibly know what she's asking.

But he answers. "A bigger home for you, of course! You're too big for the cage Pete's got. And Mom says I need to get a cage before I even *think* of bringing home a bird." Fritz chooses a book and sets it on the desk next to him. "Huh. *The Mashed Potato and Other Savory Steps: How Cuisine Impacts Dance Culture*. Weird." His fingers begin clicking away, and he gasps.

"A hundred dollars—that's an expensive book! Wow!" He grabs another. "Fifty-two fifty?"

Aggie flutters her wings excitedly, her eyes shining like two elderberries. "Did you hear that? He's getting us a home, Alastair! We'll be a real family in our own home!"

I feel my feathers ruffle. I dig at a messy spot on my chest and try to fix it. "A cage in Pete's isn't a home," I tell Aggie, my beak full of feathers. "And *you* and *I* are family. The two of us. Fritz split us apart, remember?"

"You know, Fritz and you are a lot alike," Aggie says dreamily, "both working so hard to get us a home . . ."

Uh . . .

". . . And you're both so smart and handsome . . ."

Um.

"You're like *twins*, Alastair!"

I love my sister. I do.

If Aggie's the sun, then I'm the rain. If she's a rose, I'm a thorn. If she's a cherry, well, I guess I'd be the pit.

I suppose there are worse things to be than a cherry pit. (Like maybe a gerbil.)

But there's definitely something wrong with her.

Sure, she isn't coughing as much as she used to. And her feathers are looking quite nice, I have to say. But rational thinking?

Hasn't been Aggie's strongest suit of late.

With statements like:

"I love the way he blows his nose, don't you?"

"Look at how he hides that bag of Cheese Please! cheesy puffs in his backpack! Storing away food for the dry season—what a good bird!"

"It's a kind heart that doesn't mind when you poop on his favorite shirt."

—I'd say it's pretty clear she's gone just shy of crazy. The sooner I separate the two lovebirds, the better. So . . .

I've been hatching a plan.

A real live, actual plan. To escape. I figure we'll bust out of here through the air vent in the ceiling. Or Aggie's getting pretty good at chewing through wood lately. I could sign her up to chew a hole in the door. Then we'll fly off to a tree—maybe a kola nut. Or I always thought I'd like a pine. Dark and prickly, just like me.

No—a palm.

Aggie says Pete's got a poster behind the register: miles of turquoise sea, palm trees, and the bluest sky you've ever seen. Porky says the place in the picture's Key West. A place called Florida.

Probably a few flaps of the wings, tops.

It should all be quite simple, really. Birds have made an art out of flying in its many forms, after all. Ever heard about the chicken who "flew the coop"?

Escape comes as natural as a pair of wings.

(And as soon as my bad wing heals, escape shouldn't be a problem. Honest. I have absolutely no concerns that it's been four weeks and the wing's got a bit of a bend in it and hurts when I flap. No concerns whatsoever.)

I leave the irritating feathers on my chest alone and walk the short distance to Aggie and begin to preen her affectionately. I'm making a point. Aggie and me? We're the same breed, the same species: human-parrot, parrot-human—whatever it is, we're the same.

"Forget Fritz," I say.

I see Aggie's feathers fluff a little, and those elderberry eyes narrow ever so slightly. "No, Alastair, you're wrong. Fritz *is* family," she says.

Just then Fritz pipes up from his place at the glowing box. "I'll get you out of here. With money like this, I'll have you home in no time." He swivels his chair and looks at Aggie. "Mom and Fiona are gonna love you. Just like I do."

Aggie looks away from him and back to me. "Family loves you and looks out for you"—her voice is solemn—"and keeps loving you and looking out for you, no matter what. *That's* family. And Fritz is part of ours."

Not if I can help it.

I stomp across the room to the desk and find a

fleshy spot above Fritz's ankle. And I chomp. Hard.

Fritz howls. Aggie howls. I hold fast.

My beak has a mind of its own, and it slices into Fritz's thumb as he tries to swat me away. And in one fleeting thought, I wonder if this might not be the best idea. I mean, I'm so close. So close to finally living with Aggie in the shop . . .

But then I think of Fritz taking Aggie home with him. Away. From me.

Forever.

You know, flying with a bum wing is a lot harder than it looks.

But catapulted across the room, you get a good head start . . .

Until you hit a concrete sack of dog food.

I wake and look down at a bandage on my good side. Not again.

My *second* broken wing.

Medical Log, July 25

- Age: 12 years 20 days
- Weight: Same, I think
- Height: I think I grew?
- Current status: Ingrown toenail

Fiona came to the shop today. She said she talked to Dad on the phone. I must have bbbeen at work or something. I haven't talked to him since my bbbbirthday, when I told him I wished he were here to celebrate . . . and then I cried a little . . . and then he got mad and said it wasn't his fault. That was three weeks ago. I didn't mean to make him feel bbbbbad.

Maybbbbe the phone company's just bbbbeen dropping his calls lately.

Or, maybbbe I'm *always* at work when Dad calls. Maybbbbe that's it. Maybbbbbe he keeps calling, and I accidentally miss it every time.

Fiona gave me lots of bbbbooks. That was nice.

Mom's working late. Again. I hate that she had to get another jobbbb. It's always bbbetter when she only has one.

Alastair bbbbit me today. Twice. First he got me on the ankle. When I reached down to get him loose, he grabbbbbbbbbbbbbed onto my thumbbbb. He was really attached, so I shook him. Then I shook him some more. And then I was a little worried I'd need stitches, so I kinda flung him. Just like Pete. I still can't bbbbbelieve I did that. I can still see him flying through the air.

I really thought I was going to help Alastair.

BBBut like everything else, I messed that up too.

I miss Grandpa.

Signed: Dr. F

PS Sorry. The bbbandage on my thumbbbb keeps getting caught in the *bbbbbbbbb* key.

CHAPTER 7

*I*f a bird with a broken wing is a cliché . . .

Then I'm a full-blown catastrophe.

My little biting escapade earned me another four weeks in the Infirmary, hurling all my plans across the shop, where they've broken apart and lie in pieces on the floor. Every time I think of it, I want to take a feather in my beak and rip it out.

Not like a feather picker or anything.

Just . . . as a bit of relief.

Never mind. Forget I said that.

To add insult to my injury, Pete cut Fritz's hours now that we need less hand-feeding, and Aggie visits only twice a day. I miss her. And I haven't had a moment's peace since Porky got back from Mrs. Plopky's new social club. He's spent a full week in the spa to "recuperate," and since I'm the only one back here, he's got no one to talk to but yours truly.

"A pig's got no business wearing a tutu! A TUTU!" has been his daily lament, followed by worries the shop and Babs in particular will find out. "A pink skirt. Just like that one," he adds, closing his eyes and pointing a tiny claw to the wall calendar and a picture of a potbellied pig dressed as a ballerina. "It'll be my ruination." (It would seem he isn't too worried about my take on his fashion fiasco.)

But finally, by summer's end, as the mercury soars and Porky's tutu troubles fade into the distant past, my second wing decides it's going to heal. The first broken wing, on the other hand—well, that's a topic I won't discuss further, because there are bigger goldfish to fry.

Fiona's castoffs have been a gold mine, and Fritz has managed to save enough money for a used birdcage taller than him and plans to erect it in the shop, where Aggie and I will be officially up for sale by the end of the week. "Should be here by Friday!" Fritz informs us when he arrives later that day. "Just in time for Alastair to move in. For real this time."

He's also bought a battery-powered, handheld fan that he hasn't put down in days. "Catching a breeze is about as likely as catching cholera these days. Why's it gotta be so hot?" he whines, and takes a long swig from the orange Fizzy Pop holstered to his belt. "As a pre-premed student, I know I shouldn't be drinking this. The sugar alone could send me into diabetic shock—but a person can only drink so much water."

He collapses onto the cool floor, tears a towel he's fashioned into a headband from his head, and rockets it in the direction of the basket Pete uses for the shop's soiled towels and blankets. It misses.

Aggie, who's been visiting three hamsters with colds Fritz brought to the Infirmary this afternoon, climbs down the shelving, beak to foot, beak to foot, and flops onto the floor. She waddles over to Fritz's towel and takes it in her beak.

"Get it, Aggie!" Fritz cheers. "Make your basket!"

"Go! Go! Go! Go!" chant the hamsters in tiny

voices, but they dissolve into fits of coughing.

Beside Pete's laundry basket, Fritz has placed an empty fishbowl. He'd spent a few days teaching Aggie to fetch any small pieces of laundry that have missed their mark, and now Aggie obediently gathers all hand towels and blanket shreds (courtesy of the puppies) and drops them inside.

I can hardly abide it.

If she weren't so proud of herself, I'd put a stop to it. But I won't, no matter how much I hate it. No matter how ghastly the cause of her present happiness. Because all ghastly things must come to an end. And that end is coming soon.

Aggie deposits the sweaty towel in the bowl and receives praise and her new favorite treat, a cashew, from Fritz. She's positively aglow as she bobs over to me. "That's so fun," she sings. "You really should try it. I'm working on my beak muscles, so I can pick up bigger stuff like blankets. Fritz said laundry service will be part of my chores when I—"

"Aggie," I interrupt. "Aggie, do you remember what Fritz said?"

"What Fritz said about what?"

I'm beginning to think Aggie doesn't understand the gravity of our situation. A sales sticker means that we could be separated anytime, could go home with anybody. I've got a pretty good scheme in place to toss a few sunflower seeds at the wall of fish aquariums Aggie's told me about, breaking the glass and riding the wave out of the shop, but I don't think Aggie's taken my latest escape plan seriously. (Her comment, *Forever's not long enough to spend with you and Fritz, but at least I have a lifetime,* may have tipped me off.) I clear my throat and try to sound comforting. "You know, what Fritz says will happen at twelve weeks."

"Oh, yes, I know."

She obviously doesn't. I try again. "Aggie, you do remember Pete wants to sell us, don't you?" I wince, hoping it didn't come out too harsh, and wait for tears.

Aggie climbs onto the wooden swing Fritz installed for her here in the storeroom and swings back and forth, happily attacking a wood block.

"Ag, he wants to *sell* us."

Aggie stops pecking the block and stares at me. She blinks. "I'm *aware*, Alastair," she says. "Pete's *going* to sell us. . . ."

Mm-hmmmm.

She flaps her wings. "Sell us to Fritz!"

Ooooh boy.

"Fritz told me, Alastair! He said he's saving his money—look, it's in his bank!"

I look to where Fritz's bank, a replica of the human heart, sits on the desk, leaking bills. There's money there, sure, but even if Aggie's right, even if Fritz *is* expecting to buy us, it doesn't take a genius to figure out a cage and all those PARROT CROSSING stickers he's bought recently must've eaten into his stash.

"He said as soon as he has enough, he's going to plunk that money down—that's what he said—and then we'll be together forever," Aggie adds, clasping her wings to her chest.

And just then something begins to worm its way into my mind.

Now, Fritz will lie as fast as look at you. Says something about a "proper cage cleaning" and pulls the poop papers right out from under you. I can't tell you how many times he's come up to me and asked, "Polly want a cracker?"

There are never any crackers.

I ate his "science" report on cherry trees. *Cherry trees?*

Listen, I've got a good instinct about trees. Pines, I know. Palm—got it. But cherry?

Nope.

And since when is on instinct wrong, I ask you? Besides, nothing that perfect just leaps from the ground. Perfect things don't just happen. Perfection takes planning, *brains.*

Fritz's talk of buying us might be just like the rest, a string of lies and fairy tales, but now, as I listen to Aggie's story about Fritz's careful saving, the thought wriggling around my mind makes its way down, curls up in the pit of my stomach.

Fritz *is* planning on buying a bird.

One bird.

And it's Aggie.

With enough time and diligence, he just may be

able to do it. He'd been dangling this fish story about the two of us, and Aggie ate it up. Hook, line, and sinker.

"Here you go, Alastair," Fritz says, interrupting my thoughts and plopping a large, softbound book in front of me. "This was left over from my garage sale," he continues. "Sorry about all the water damage. It's good enough to rip up, though. You want it?" He waits a moment as if expecting a thank-you. Instead I turn my back to him to study a particularly thrilling knot in the pine flooring.

I will not be bought, you see.

A customer rings the bell out on the sales floor.

"Come on, Aggie. Let's see who it is," I hear Fritz say.

"Welcome to Pete's Pet (and Parrot!) Shack! How can we help you?" Aggie squawks, not in words any human could understand, of course, but in the language of birds. Our language.

I turn around in time to watch Fritz place her on his shoulder, and the two of them head into the store to answer the bell.

All of it needles my growing pinfeathers. Makes

me itchy. I look down to angrily rearrange a few feathers and see the book.

Hm.

Here's the problem: I've already shredded the last of Fritz's school papers, and I've had a hankering for anything lined, typed, printed, or bound for a good week now. At this point a sticky note would do.

I listen as a muffled Fritz begins chirping away about flea combs. I try to interest myself in that knot on the floor, but I can still see the book out of the corner of my eye.

What'll it hurt? I just need a taste.

I cave and poke my beak into a few of the curled pages. The water damage has puffed and feathered them, but even so, I notice they're thinner, airier than most. The pages crinkle as I nudge them, and I try one last time to control myself.

But Fritz knows my weakness. The lure is too much.

I tear out a single sheet and begin to gnaw at it.

Cue the angels.

On First Biting into Norton's Anthology[1]

Much have I tasted in the reams[2] of white,
And many cable bills all long since due;
Through many yellow phone books have I chewed
With beak of iron strength and awful might.
Through thus, this printed tripe,[3] did I then bite,
And twaddle in scores to justly conclude
That all was scribbled garbage, foul and crude,
Till I nipped Norton, and all became light:
Then felt I like some thresher of the wheat
Who grinds his grain for finest feel and taste;
Or like some baker when by flour and sweet
He stumbles on bread seemingly heaven-traced—
Snowflakes of manna[4] from firmament's[5] seat—
That melt on tongues, dew-frosted, honey-laced.

---

1. An unexpectedly sweet (and spicy) regurgitation. Inspired by John
   Keats's poem "On First Looking into Chapman's Homer."
2. reams: large quantities of paper.
3. tripe: worthless writing.
4. manna: bread from heaven. (I ate a biblical account of it. Bread that tastes
   like honey and falls to the ground like dew? I'll take two helpings.)
5. firmament: blue, blue sky.

CHAPTER 8

I tolerated the odd worksheet. I tried my beak at a few pages on gut bacteria.

I drool over poetry.

Something about the way a poem tickles the taste buds, blooming in the mouth, taking on flavor after flavor the longer you roll it around. I've found my beak can't tear poems to bits like it might a pizza box or a parrot pamphlet. I've never had a problem cracking a nutshell, feeling for its weakest point with just the tip of my tongue, but I can't crack a poem for hours. It's just a dash of words, a sprinkle of sentences, but I'm forced to savor it slowly. And savor it I do.

But here's the craziest thing:

I feel like Fritz when he watches that Letizia Tortelloni on the glowing box. She'll be chopping garlic or throwing noodles at the wall and shouting, *"Perfetto!"* and Fritz will say, "Hey! I could do that!" or, "I betcha if you dipped it in grape jelly, it'd be even better!"

I might be dipping into a little poetry snack myself and find myself thinking, *Huh. I could whip up something like this.* Or maybe I've eaten and digested a poem a week ago, and, like a light, appealing belch after eating a bowlful of peppers, it comes back to me.

I check the poem's flavor. I season it with a few words of my own. I might add a little spice to Keats, a little zing to Tennyson.

Shakespeare's got a pretty good recipe to work with. Today, Fritz has bought Aggie a new harness, so he can take her outside. Without thinking, I say, "To bite, or not to bite—that is the question."

Isn't that always the question.

But not for long. Fritz has no idea of the lengths I'll go to for my sister.

I mean it now. Distraction's over.

In addition to poetry, I've taken the liberty of altering a little Latin for you:

Fritz: *Homo sapiens*. Latin for "wise man."

But perfection takes planning, remember? *Brains.*

Alastair: *Psittacus homo sapiens erithacus.* Parrot-man of the wiser African grey sort.

Perfetto.

Dear Everett,

I was beginning to think my ringer was broke. After my guinea-pig get-together, I didn't talk to a single soul for the rest of the week. And then some. That telephone's been silent as a stone.

It was this morning when it finally rang. And guess who should call but our long-lost son!

I tell you, Everett, he's getting to be a busybody.

Remember how I told you he's been nagging me to move down to Key West, near him and the family? Says I'll love the palm trees? Just won't get it in his head this old bird doesn't want to fly away from Shirley River and everything I know?

Well, I got an earful again. Henry said I shouldn't be living alone. Said I shouldn't

be driving. (So I bumped a curb or two!)
Delores Greenbush's son told him I started a
conga line at the church picnic, and he said I
shouldn't be doing that, either.

Worries I'll break a hip, he does.

Now get this. Then the boy says he's got
a plan to move me, says he'll help pay for
it even. Where, you guess? Into the Prickly
Pines with the gals.

I wonder where he got that idea.

(Her name's Irma, and she likes kitten
stamps.)

Everett. Now, I know my friends love their
Friday night cards and their afternoon yoga.
And those social dances do seem mighty
fine (you know how I love to dance). But I
cannot, will not ever leave our home. How
could I? And leave your flower boxes? Move
your toothbrush from the holder?

Nope. I just won't do it. No sirree! You'll
have to move that toothbrush yourself, and
that's the end of it.

Besides, I can look after myself here and
don't need anyone badgering me about
taking my pills or giving up my canned peas.
Nobody's going to tell me what to do. I'm
free as a bird.

And I got a few plans of my own.

First, I signed my name up for one of those hippy-hoppy dance classes down at the community center. Last week's senior social didn't work as well as I thought. The guinea pig nearly kicked the bucket soon as I put a tutu on him. I guess rodents have real strong opinions about their fashion choices. I'll change the name and start it back up when I'm ready.

Which leads me to number two: I'm considering a new pet. Maybe a bird. I got the stamina for it. I always did think I'd enjoy having one, and who knows what poor little bird is out there that could use my company?

Yours,
Bertie

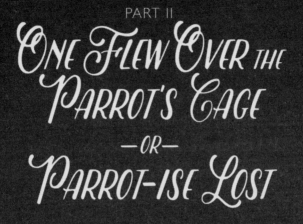

PART II

One Flew Over the Parrot's Cage
—or—
Parrot-ise Lost

CHAPTER 9

 h, my pretties!" says Pete the moment
Aggie and I are installed in our new digs.
He rubs his hands together greedily. "Ready to make
ol' Pete a buckaroo or two?"

Our cage, festooned with perches and toys of
every sort, is parked in the middle of the shop next
to several rows of metal shelves holding things like
canned dog food and dandruff shampoo. There's a
wall of fish that lines one side of the shop. The puppies have a pen on the floor. Kittens and bunnies get
the front windows, as people are more likely to come
inside if they fall in love through the glass, Aggie
tells me. Off in a back corner, the rest of the shop's

birds blather on, a cacophony of chirps, chirrups, squeaks, and squawks, every one of them trying to talk over the noise of the bird next to him, and all of them packed together on a single wooden perch. In a cage with forty birds, the last place you want to be is on the bottom rung.

Across from us, several walls of glass house every type of rodent and tortoise, and the oddball hermit crab. And once again, I'm staring into the fat and furry face of Porky, patriarch and guinea pig extraordinaire.

"Hey there, buddy!" Porky says. He's recovered from the whole tutu ordeal. It was touch and go there for a while.

There's a siege of fur, and Porky's quickly enveloped. His head pops up over the roiling mass. "Meet the kids, Alastair! Right there's Lentil; Bean's over there—we pigs always name our young'uns after eats, you know. And this here's the missus! The McPorksters, at your service!"

I wave. Sort of.

Porky cups a small hand next to his mouth

and whispers to me in his wheezy way. "The wife's name's *Tuna*, so you know, but it's a sore subject. Just call her missus." He winks.

Beside me, Aggie squeals. "Oh, Alastair! There are so many animals you still need to meet!" She proceeds to introduce me to every furred, scaled, and feathered thing in the place. ". . . and that's Harriet, that's Gloria, and you know Babs." I spot Babs and a few other familiar rabbit faces. They're surrounded by their fleet of fuzzy youngsters.

"I think that's it!" Aggie says. "Do you have everyone's names straight?"

I wasn't exactly listening. I'm too distracted, bowled over by what lies *outside* the window since the moment I entered the shop.

Trees. Leaves quaking in the warm afternoon breezes. Sunlight splashing over a brick building and winking off its windows. And in one tiny corner of the store's front window, the bluest blue I've ever seen.

The sky.

Pete's is located on a busy street, and at any one time I witness cars fighting for parking spots, window-shoppers tripping over cracks in the pavement, and sparrows stalking the hot dog cart. Aggie says she loves the balloon man.

"Pretty great, isn't it?" she asks.

I just swallow hard and continue to take in that tiny patch of blue.

"And look! There's another glowing box behind the register," Aggie says. "I have watched *lots* of episodes of *Taste of Tortelloni*. Pete likes *Port Luna Love*. Fritz says soap operas are dumb, though."

It's a lot to take in. Between the trees, the sky, and finally being reunited with my sister for the foreseeable future, I'm downright giddy.

I didn't know that was possible.

"It's Monday!" Aggie squawks.

We're deep into September before my eyes stop spinning and things start to focus. The distraction outside the window's worn off, and the remains of my *Norton Anthology* is sitting over there behind the register, where Fritz left it the day we moved in. A blob of duck sauce from one of Pete's takeout containers oozes down the binding and plops onto the counter.

"It's Monday!" Aggie squawks again. "You know what that means!"

I do know what this means. Mondays equal more of the same: puppies wiggling, mealworms wriggling, and gerbils giggling (wickedly). Pete will arrive at the shop (late). Customers will come and buy (but mostly not). And children will run to and fro throughout the store, screeching, making faces, and pointing their fat, baby-carrot fingers every which way and asking to take home every last goldfish and tailless lizard in the place. (They never ask for me. Seems they get the picture soon as I snap my beak at their tasty-looking fingers.)

Oh, and Fritz will be in. I assume that's what Aggie means.

I play along. "What's it mean, Aggie?" I ask.

"FRITZ!" Aggie screams. "Fritz-Fritz-Fritz . . . FRITZ!"

Sigh.

Aggie bobs her head. "Four p.m. That's when

he'll be here! Four p.m. every Monday, Wednesday, and Friday!"

Fritz is back at school, which means we're back to the old Fritz schedule. He tried to come in that first Saturday. Told Pete he was just picking up some crickets for Charles. But when he hadn't left after four hours, Pete told him he needed to "stop *haranguing* around that parrot cage—customers'll think you're buying. 'Sides, you're covering up the price tag." Pete wound up banning him from the shop on weekends if he wanted to keep his job.

While I've been twiddling my feathers, Aggie's been busying herself between Fritz visits. She's spent the last few days naming all the fish in the shop. Fish don't often get names. For a pet that's sold at twenty-nine cents a pop, looks exactly like the guy next to him, and, if we're being honest, appears a bit *dull*, no one thinks it's worth the trouble—except Aggie. There are so many she's gone through the alphabet twelve times over, even after assigning each name three times (Arnie #1, Arnie #2, Arnie #3, Bernie #1, Bernie #2 . . .). She's also chewed Pete's weight in wooden toys.

"I chewed up five for Fritz today," Aggie is saying. "I think that one in the corner looks like his nose, don't you? He will be so happy."

"That's some good art there," agrees Porky. "That one there really does look like the old schnozola."

I give him a withering look.

"What?" he says. "It does."

"See?" says Aggie. "Told you."

Fritz comes in for his shift, first stopping to fawn over Aggie and admire her gifts. Each time he passes our cage, Aggie follows him to the end of her perch, this way and that, her eyes holding him like a cup.

By the end of the day, Fritz manages to sell a few goldfish.

"Oh, that's a good job, Fritz!" Aggie calls out to him. "Good-bye, Carl number two! Good-bye, Arthur number three!"

"Hey, Aggie," Fritz calls to her before he leaves. "I'll be back Wednesday, okay? And don't worry—I've been doing some leaf raking and lawn mowing. I'll make that money somehow!"

We all know what he needs that money for. It

starts with an *A* and does not end with *lastair*.

But I'll let you in on a little secret.

All this distraction-free time has given me the chance to put a few new escape plans into place. I'm pretty impressed with the quality, actually. I'm not making a whole lot of progress yet, but we'll see which one pans out.

Plan A: Gnaw through cage bars. Once out, Aggie and I attach to customer's hat like some artistic ornament. Flounce out of store. (Estimated timetable: Being that I've made no progress on the bars, that part's a little fuzzy.)

Plan B: Wait for small child to open cage. Restrain self from biting fat carrot fingers. Crawl into small child's Perry Panda backpack to be smuggled out. (Estimated timetable: unknown, as I haven't yet been able to restrain myself from nipping.)

Plan C (and this is the most probable): Wait for someone to pick one of Pete's plastic yogurt spoons out of the garbage and drop it into our cage. Dig tunnel with spoon (tunnel hidden by poop papers).

Fly to freedom on unclipped, unbent wing. Live happily feathered after. (Estimated timetable: The wing should heal any minute now.)

Freedom: I can taste it.

CHAPTER 10

September drifts into October; October blows into November. I pay no attention to the jangling bell on the door anymore. Honestly, I don't even hear it.

I'm still waiting for somebody to drop a plastic spoon in my cage.

Today, however, I can't help but notice when a short, round figure presses through the shop door and promptly tears the bell from its hinge.

"Oh my," a familiar voice tuts.

Fritz is working, and as he rounds the corner, the figure points in the direction of the bell. It's clattered to a stop in front of the puppy pen. The puppies, as you'd expect, have lost their minds.

"I'm sorry, dear. I'm not sure what happened. I simply walked through the door, and off it popped! I'm such a klutz!"

Fritz gathers the bell from the floor. "Don't worry, ma'am," he says. "I'm sure Pete can fix it."

The woman's back is to me as she unties a scarf protecting her silvery curls. I spot a pink curler. "You're a peach. Is Peter here, dear?"

Fritz nods his head and points a thumb toward the back room. "Inventory. He says I gotta man the shop. Can I interest you in a newt? Christmas is just around the corner. Nothing says 'happy holidays' like a newt!" The old woman turns around.

It's Mrs. Plopky. Puppy borrower. Costumer of guinea pigs. Her cheeks are pushed up into two plump pillows, and she chuckles in a way that reminds me of the purple martins that once nested in the tree outside the shop's window. "Oh no, dear. No newts today. I'm just here to pick up . . ."

She opens her pocketbook, selects a scrap of paper from a paper-clipped stack, and lifts a pair of spectacles, fastened to a thin chain around her neck, to her nose. "Some fish food for Humpty Dumpty," she reads. "And a satin cat cushion—my Tiger can be so particular."

"Right this way," Fritz answers. He leads her around the shop, suggesting not only these fish flakes and that pillow, but a few toys, a scratching tower, and a beach-ball-size bowl for her goldfish. "I'm sure Humpty Dumpty will love this one. The glass is tempered, so it won't break easy."

"My, yes!" she exclaims. "I'm certain he will! You do know a lot about this shop, now, don't you?" She reaches a wrinkled hand out to Fritz. "My name's Bertie. Bertie Plopky. It's a pleasure to meet such a polite young man."

Fritz shakes her hand a little too forcefully, so that her entire body jiggles with each pump. "It's nice to meet you, too. You look a little familiar. . . . Well, anyway, the name's Fritz." He proceeds to tell her about his acute knowledge of everything pet-shop related. Ever predictable, he follows this up with his life goals.

I, on the other hand, continue to watch this old woman. Something about the way she shuffles up and down the aisles following Fritz reminds me of Aggie. Even the way her hair is perfectly curled in those neat rolls, tight around her face, and then sparks up in back like forked lightning. Aggie's feathers never sit down either. I find myself leaning in, eyes pinned to her.

"Do you have any pets, dear?"

"Oh, yes," answers Fritz. "I have a newt named Charles. He's a really good newt. People don't realize how loving newts can be. And I'm buying a bird—"

"A bird?" Bertie asks, sounding surprised.

"Yep!" says Fritz, proud as a peacock.

"Why, me too! That's the real reason I came in here!"

Fritz's beams. "I can help you with that! What kind of bird were you thinking? We've got finches and canaries, and we've got forty parakeets to choose from."

I take a step forward and accidentally tip over a bowl of pellets; they spill and go rat-a-tat-tatting over the shop floor.

"What kind is that?"

I look up to see Bertie pointing at me and Aggie.

Fritz's eyes widen. "Uh, well . . ."

"Tell me: Are birds like that friendly?" asks Bertie.

"Um, I . . ."

Bertie shuffles toward our cage. Fritz follows, looking very worried all of a sudden.

"Lovely, just lovely. See the way this one's perched—a gentleman of a bird if I ever saw one! Looks to have a stinker streak, though." She's eyeballing me, but there's no hint of recognition. Age and the full coat of feathers has thrown her off. She turns her attention to Aggie. "And this one! What a gem!"

"That's Aggie," a pale Fritz says.

"And the stinker?"

"I named him Alastair," says Fritz. "I raised them both. I even fixed Alastair's broken wing when Pete tossed him."

I beg to differ. That one still hurts.

Bertie whistles through her teeth and sets a wrinkled hand on Fritz's shoulder. "My, my—you *are* a bright boy. You'll make a great doctor one day—I'm certain of it." She takes a step closer to my cage and fixes her bifocals on me. "A broken wing, you say."

"Actually, two."

"*Two* broken wings?"

A parakeet twitters from his cage. "Guy's a poor excuse for a bird," he tells the neighbors sandwiched next to him. "You see that wing? Looks like the puppies got to it."

I shrink a little and look around to see if anyone else was listening.

Bertie goes on. "Well, we are all a little beat up now, aren't we? I've got heaps of afflictions myself. Just look at these liver spots." She points to a field of small gray puddles on her hands. "These hands used to be white as bridal silk! Soft like it too. Everett always said that."

"Who's Everett?" Fritz asks.

"Oh, well now—" Bertie stops and grips Fritz's shoulder. "Everett's my husband."

"Does he like birds?"

Bertie's eyes twinkle behind the rims of her glasses, and the chain clinks merrily as she laughs. "Lord, no! He's a pill! Loves poetry and gardening and that's it! Otherwise, he's a bit of a grump." She winks at Fritz. "Made him dance with me, though. Foxtrot, jitterbug, polka—all of it. Do you dance?"

Fritz shakes his head. "Oh, no, ma'am. I'm terrible at it. My feet always trip me up."

"Oh, that doesn't matter," Bertie says, waving her hands side to side and tapping a foot. "I'm a klutz myself, but that never stopped me. You keep dancing like you don't give a fig, and no one pays any mind to your stumbles. All those ballerinas and such, they envy us wobblier folks. You can have a lot more fun when you quit caring what you look like."

"Maybe you're right—"

"I am right! Back in my day I could get a whole gymnasium of people boppin' their socks off. I found my Everett at a dance. He couldn't take his eyes off me."

"Wow."

"Wow, yes! That man never danced a step in

his life until that day. But he followed me out on that dance floor and never looked back," Bertie says. "You know, you remind me of him a little. My Everett wanted to be a doctor once. Couldn't afford the schooling, though." She grabs Fritz's chin with two fingers and gives it a little shake. "You be a doctor, young Fritz. You got it in you."

Fritz nods his head, and his lower lip quivers just a little.

Pete scuffles in from the back room and notices his one customer straightaway. He rakes his hands through his greasy hair and groans. "This here's a pet store, Mrs. Plopky, not a rent-a-pet."

"Oh, Peter." Bertie waves him away. "No, no. I was just speaking with this sweet young man you have working for you. He's trying to interest me in one of these birds."

Fritz swallows. "Uh, well, I, not rea—"

"Oho! He is, is he?" Pete interrupts, clearly interested in this turn of events. "Did Fritz tell you all the benefits of owning parrots? Fascinating stuff. I think it's here in one of these books. . . ." Pete starts half-heartedly thumbing through one of the yellowed parrot manuals he has for sale. "Page sixty-eight, I'm pretty sure." He keeps looking up to see if Bertie is waiting for him to show her.

"Never mind about that, Peter," she says, patting his hand. "What I'd really like to know is: Do they make good companions? My Tiger wants nothing to do with me. And Humpty, well he's a bit of a cold fish. I guess that must be about right for a goldfish, but I would like something a little more, you know . . . *loving*?"

"How about a guinea pig?" suggests Fritz.

Pete gives him a strange look. "I do believe we're talking about a parrot, Fritz my boy." Pete gestures to the rest of the parrot books on the rack. "All these books here say that parrots are wonderful companions—like loving children, really."

"But Alastair's crabby," adds Fritz.

Bertie hooks an eye on me, more intently than before. "Crabby?"

Pete claps Fritz on the back. "*Heh-heh-heh*, I wouldn't say crabby—unloved! Just a little depressed—needs someone to love him! And then there's the other one—"

Bertie waves a hand in Pete's direction. "Crabby doesn't bother me so much—I'm used to crabby! Crabby doesn't always mean you can't enjoy someone's company."

"They'll give you company, no doubt about it," assures Pete. "Did you know greys can talk?"

"Do they!"

"Oh, but these don't," says Fritz.

"Well, not just yet!" says Pete, giving Fritz a stern look. "But they'll learn. You can teach 'em, Mrs. Plopky!"

"Doesn't matter one way or the other," says Bertie.

"Aggie's sick!" shouts Fritz. "And who knows? She may not live long. I've heard of avian cancers that'll—"

"Cancers!" yells Pete. "Poppycock! This bird will outlive you, Mrs. Plopky. Can live a good sixty years! Maybe more!"

Bertie furrows her brow. She steps close enough for me to see the bright blue of her eyes behind her glasses and the almost disappearing lashes. "Well, now, that could be upsetting. None of us will live forever, and I wouldn't want to leave such a lovely creature to live who knows where else after my passing."

"You don't worry your pretty little head about a thing like that," Pete says. "Fritz here will ring you up for those birds there. They'll be true friends—you'll see."

The parakeet in the back pipes up again. "Buy one, get the broken one free!"

Aggie hears him this time and whips her head around to try to spot the little brute, while I straighten my back and cross my feathers again that no one else heard.

"Cash or charge?" Pete presses.

Bertie hesitates. "Maybe I should think on it a little more."

"Yes! You should! She's awfully expensive!" Fritz shouts, and receives another slap on the back from Pete.

"I always say, you can't put a price on friendship." Bertie looks at the price tag, adjusts her glasses, and gulps. "But I will think on it." She pats Fritz's cheek. "You boys have helped me so. Your mothers should be proud."

My eyes follow her out of the store. "Toodle-oo!" she calls as she steps outside onto the blustery sidewalk. Leaves spin down the street.

Fritz looks down at the fishbowl in his hands. "She was so worried about a bird, she forgot her things," he whispers. And a cold gust of air sneaks in as the door swings shut and sends a chill up my spine.

"I'm docking you a day's pay, kid," says Pete once Mrs. Plopky's out of sight. "You mighta lost me a big sale." He walks to the back room, scowling as he goes.

Fritz sniffs, rubs his nose on his sleeve, and gives Aggie a sad look. "Don't worry, girl. Just means one extra day, that's all."

Aggie says nothing, only coughs and hangs her head.

Medical Log, November 8

- Age: 12 years 4 months
- Weight: 119.9 lbs
- Height: 53 in
- Current status: Insomnia, trouble breathing, increased sweat production, weight loss, 4 stress pimples, 1 ingrown toenail

Dear Medical Log,

Holy dyspepsia.

My current medical status says it all. I am stressed. How am I going to do this???

I just counted the money I have left in my cardiac bank, checked under the sofa cushions and in Grandpa's old register in the food truck, and cleaned out every last coin spot in Mom's car. (I found $7.92 and a Toaster Tart.) I even checked all my old birthday cards in case I missed something (a cat hair, that was about it).

I came up with a grand total of: $731.14. Not bad for a seventh grader!

But, by my calculations, that means I'm still $568.86 short.

It's times like this I wish we were back in the Fry Guys food truck. I'd sit on the ice cream cooler like I used to, and Grandpa would be cooking up chicken fingers and French fries, and I'd tell him everything, and he'd listen, really listen, and by the time the fries were just perfect—not too bendy and not too crispy—he'd know what to do.

If it was something like memorizing some medical terminology, I'd just make some flash cards.

Or if it was just about getting the money, I'd only need time.

But it's not simple like that. Right now, all I do is worry about the things that could go wrong. For example:

What if someone tries to buy Aggie before I can? What if someone BAD tries to buy her? What if it just takes FOREVER to save that much money, and I wind up with an anxiety condition?

Or, what if Aggie gets sick like she was when she was a baby? Something's not right; I can tell. I thought she was just missing me lately, and that kind of made me feel happy. But I found out Pete's been feeding her hot dogs. Then I saw a peanut in her dish! Those can be toxic!

I know what Letizia Tortelloni would probably say about it. She'd say, *Ah, you take a chance. You mix the anchovy with the cheese, the pistachio with the peas. Who knows what you get? You try.* Perfetto!

She'd say I should just work at saving, try to help Aggie, see what happens.

But that's what I'm scared of. Sometimes, what happens is:

Kids laugh at you. Like when you agree to go to basketball camp because your mom wants you to meet some new friends, but you keep tripping on the court because she bought your sneakers a little big so you could grow into them.

Or you end up crying in the bathroom during

seventh period because you wrote a whole list of ideas on how to get your dad to move back, and after James and the kids at your lunch table tell you they won't work, you go to the office to call your mom because you need to know if they're right, and by the way she sounds when she answers your questions, you realize he's never coming home.

Sometimes you might break a parrot's wing.

Or a person could be sitting next to you. You're getting some practice filling out a medical chart, and he's talking to you about the time he was flipping burgers and a squirrel ran right up and got caught in his pant leg. And you tell yourself he's probably just tired and needs a nap, because he can't even talk right. But later, you watch from your window as a bunch of paramedics load him into an ambulance and drive away.

Sometimes it's the bad things that happen. My stomach hurts just thinking about it.

I tried explaining all of this to Fiona. But she just handed me one of those little slips of paper you get in fortune cookies that said *He who worries best changes nothing.*

I mean, I sorta get what the fortune means. I get that there's no use worrying about something that might never happen. But it doesn't make me feel better.

I think I'll try to swing by the shop with some healthy food for Aggie later. I'll just tell Pete I'm buying some crickets for Charles.

I'm pretty sure I can stuff a pound of blueberries in my shorts.

Signed: Francis Feldman, MD

PS If I were Fiona, I would've traded someone for a different fortune. I like the ones that predict an egg roll in your future.

Update: Cargo shorts hold two and a half pounds of blueberries.

CHAPTER 11

"Order! Come to order! Hey! You rabbits—quit your yakking! We're trying to have a meeting here!"

Part of our new normal on the sales floor has been nightly meetings after the OPEN sign on the shop's door is turned over and Pete's gone home. Hamsters' wheels are silenced; skinks and salamanders press up against their glass enclosures to take a gander at the goings-on; birds pop their heads through cage bars. Porky presides.

"Hey—Babs!" he shouts. "We're talking adoptions over here! You'd do well to listen up!"

"Porky," groans Babs through a mouthful of

rabbit kibble. She eyes her nails. "I'm not looking all sweet anymore. I've had eighty-four kids. It takes a toll on a rabbit's figure."

Porky rolls his eyes and sighs. "If I've said it once, I've said it a million times: If you wanna get adopted, you gotta look cute and cuddly. Big eyes. Puff out those cheeks. Remember the saying: 'Skin and bone? You get no home.' Spunky and chunky is how folks like their pets! Look at your fur! You look . . . clumpy." He points in the direction of a cluster of rabbits lounging in a corner and twirling their ears. "And so do you, Gloria; you too, Harriet! If you didn't spend so much time shootin' the breeze, you might have some time to clean up a little. You got week-old carrot in your coat."

"What's 'shootin' the breeze' mean?" whispers Harriet. Gloria shrugs.

"Nothing! Never mind. The rest of you, listen up!" Porky bangs a petrified carrot-stick on the edge of his food dish. "We got six weeks to Christmas, runts, and you know what that means! Best time to get purchased. We got lots of those parents coming into the shop looking for little Johnny's puppy present and Susie's three-toed box turtle. Fluff that fur! Shine those shells! Smile! We gotta look our best, act our best, and hope for the best!"

"HURRAH!" shout the lot of them, except for the fish, who stare blankly, and the puppies, who have the attention span of a houseplant. Puppies have nothing to worry about, anyway. Customers seem to think they're nothing *but* cute, even while they take turns sniffing one another's butts.

The rest of the shop begins exchanging advice and demonstrating things like eye batting. I keep silent and pretend my toe skin is in need of some serious attention. The topics vary from how to refresh a wilted piece of spinach to ten tips on looking and smelling your buy-worthy best (tip number one: curb your turds!).

You can see why my toe skin holds appeal.

Aggie, however, raises a timid wing with a question but quickly slips it back down.

"What's up?" I ask her.

"Do you think I—I mean—well, am I looking my buy-worthy best?" she asks me.

I was waiting for this question.

I hate to say it, but Aggie *is* looking a bit ratty these days. She was fine for a while, excited to be together, live in a big cage, but as Fritz's hours dwindled and the days wore on, she stopped expecting every day would be the day Fritz would take her home. He keeps her hopes up with promises, but I'm starting to think I might be worrying about him for nothing. I've seen kids in the shop. They never have cash. That's why they're always asking for a quarter to buy a bubble-gum from the machine next to Pete's register.

I'm a little more worried about the old lady.

Still, Aggie's convinced Fritz *will* buy her, and no one but Fritz. In the meantime, she hasn't been eating, and she's chewing on her feathers. She's no feather picker, mind you, but she's definitely doing a little anxious preening lately. And then there's that cough that's back.

"It doesn't matter, Aggie," I assure her. "I'm getting us out of here, remember?"

Out of the cloud of pet shop chatter, the nasally voice from the parakeet cage butts in again. "You're not going anywhere on that chicken wing."

"Hey!" scolds Aggie, straightening herself up and frowning. "His wing's gonna heal. And my brother can do anything he puts his mind to—you mind your own business."

"Get a load of these guys!" the parakeet shouts to his buddies. "They think they're flying outta here!" Along the perch, forty parakeet heads bob with laughter.

My claws curl into the wood beneath me, and heat flares in my cheeks as I close my eyes and imagine plucking these turkeys.

Aggie turns back to me. "Don't listen to them." She clears her throat.

"So?" she asks again. "Do you think I'm buy-worthy?" She sidesteps along the perch toward me. I wince as her feathers graze my bad wing. I feel her thin bones underneath and shudder.

"Alastair, you're not answering me."

"You're the most buy-worthy bird I've ever seen," I respond, and I mean it.

Outside, the wind picks up. Little by little, the voices of hamsters and hedgehogs drift off, and just past the window, the first haunting flakes of snow begin to fall. I shouldn't know this is snow, but somehow I do.

"Wow," whispers Aggie. Her eyes spark with excitement for the first time in a long time. "Isn't it spectacular?"

"Sure is," I reply.

She sighs heavily, and the spark dims. "I wish Fritz were here to see this. He'd love it."

Another gust of wind sweeps through the sleepy street. It worries every speck of air, and we watch as the frenzied snowflakes slow, then slip down once more.

Like tears.

Aggie coughs. "Alastair?" Her voice is pinched.

"Yeah?"

"He'll have enough money soon, won't he?"

I shudder again. Once. Twice.

I know what my sister wants. She wants to hear that everything will turn out just the way she thinks

126

it will. She's got visions of cashews dancing in her head. Visions of her and Fritz and me.

"Don't worry, Aggie."

Her stomach growls, and she shivers. "He said he would. . . ." Aggie walks over to her food bowl and steps into a patch of light. It illuminates every dull feather, puts a spotlight on her thinness.

She looks at the seeds in her bowl. And walks away.

I don't want to say more.

It's not true—Fritz won't come and rescue her. That's my job. And I'm working on it. Coming up with as many plans as I can. I just haven't been successful yet. But I'm close. I know it. Like an instinct, I feel it in my bones.

Aggie coughs again, and I look over at her but have to pinch my eyes shut.

She needs all her troubles to fly off and perch somewhere else; I know this. She needs just a little crumb of hope.

I manage to get a few words out—for Aggie's sake. "If Fritz—if he said it, I'm sure he means it."

Aggie smiles weakly. "Thanks, Alastair. You're the best brother ever—you know that?" Her voice sounds small and far away.

I won't say more. I can't add another word. But something crawls into my throat, trying to wriggle its way out. I shove it back, squash it down.

Aggie coughs again, but this time she doesn't stop. The seconds near eternity; each cough sets another feather on edge.

"Sorry about that," she gasps once the spell is over. "I just get so cold sometimes. I'm sure it's nothing."

My skin weighs like iron, and every plume feels out of place, sharp, biting. I shudder one last time as I pull my sister under my bad wing and try to push away this rock, this mountain of fear. It remains, solid and unmoving.

Though it's the last thing I thought I'd ever say, I let it fall from my beak. The words come out strangled. "Aggie, you'll be home soon—home with Fritz."

To My Dear and Loving Sister[1]

If ever two could stand, then surely we.
If ever *one* could bear all strain, then thee.
If ever bird had substance, it was you;
'Twas me who proved the weaker of the two.
Let stars fall down and earth wring out her seas;
Let mountains melt like wax before the heat;
Though sun be dimmed, yet I'd know in the gloam[2],
The sky is bluest near us, for *we*'re home.
But bid me courage for this troubled day,
To brave uncertain future, come what may.
For soon I'd give thee up, bird of a feather,
If keeping you here meant loss altogether.

---

1. This concoction, inspired by Anne Bradstreet's poem "To My Dear and
   Loving Husband," boasts a distinct familial flavor and a bitter aftertaste.
2. gloam: a delicious word for twilight.

CHAPTER 12

Everyone has their moments of weakness, right? I blame it on a bad sunflower seed.

Rest assured, I am back to my normal self. It might never have happened except for a little of what I like to call "bovine intervention."

Workers came in last week and clanked around in the ceiling for a few hours, and by the time they left, the puppies were raving lunatics and the ductwork from the lab renting the space above the pet shop was connected to ours.

The lab's name is Bio-Scents.

They study the effects of cow manure on the human nose.

You get the picture.

It doesn't help that while the workers were up there tinkering with the ventilation system, they broke the furnace. The shop's been blazing at around ninety degrees for six days straight.

Heat + cow manure fumes = no customers, angry Pete . . . and a Merry Christmas to me!

The temperature outside hovers somewhere around the freezing mark, but Pete's had all the doors and windows open, trying to air the place out. He's even donned a Santa suit (i.e., cotton-ball-trimmed shorts), plastered SALE! signs everywhere, and wished upon the Christmas star that customers will brave the stink long enough to purchase that tarantula on little Tommy's and Katie's Christmas lists.

So far, his plan hasn't worked. The gerbils have begun taking bets on how few cash register rings there will be (yesterday: two) and how long a customer will stay before they run out holding their nose. Only the gerbils place bets, of course. No one wants to risk being indebted to one. Everyone knows they're in it for blood.

But as much as the rest of the store seems to wilt and retch in the heat and stench, it seems the essence of cow dung does wonders for me. Circumstances have allowed me to devise a simple, yet exceedingly clever, plan to get us out of this place and fly Aggie somewhere she'll get better—for good.

Simple, Yet Exceedingly Clever, Plan to Fly Out of Pete's Pet (and Parrot!) Shack for Good: Flap wings like crazy bird until Pete takes notice and remembers long-forgotten wing clipping. Wait for Pete to take Aggie and me out of cage for said wing clipping. Create diversion (biting has been known to work, yet this can backfire, as we all know). During commotion, Aggie slips out open front door. Create second diversion large enough for Pete to forget about me. (Remember to think of second diversion.) Strut out the front door into the hope and merriment of the December season.

Sometimes I surprise even myself.

The week before Christmas, the vents and heating are as broken as ever. Pete was well-nigh to busting a blood feather until customers started coming in anyway, braving the stink-oven to fill their stockings with dog bones and flea shampoo. Monster and Morris, two of the golden retriever puppies, left in hole-punched gift boxes, as did Fats the hamster, a boatload of hedgehogs, and kittens galore. Even Gloria found a home.

Pete's added a few chewed-up stockings to the checkout (the puppies got to them first) and a scrawny pink tree with blinking lights to the front window. Its branches are strung with leashes, collars, and a muzzle or two for cheery effect, while the Santa suit now boasts a garland and a large tinsel snowflake. The atmosphere around here is almost jolly.

"*Deck the halls with fleas and fur balls, fa la la la la, la la la la!* Got yer new aquarium right over here, Mr. Neudall. On sale, too! One forty-nine ninety-nine!" Pete hoists a large box over his head, zigzags through the aisles, and nearly trips over a little girl with a turtle in her lap.

It's a snowy Saturday morning, and, so close to Christmas, the shop is packed. Kids are running laps around the store, hopped up on candy canes, and parents are sweating the ninety-degree heat and the price tags. The puppies haven't stopped yapping all morning, and it seems every small rodent-type creature is scurrying, every bird chirping.

A particularly wily-looking boy with sandy hair and candy cane goo smeared across his face steps close to our cage. Aggie's napping—a worrisome thrice-a-day habit she's picked up—but she startles out of it. She backs up as I step closer, closing the distance between boy and sister.

"Hey, MOM! Look at this!" He pushes a thick finger between the bars of the cage and wiggles it around. There's a thin slice of dirt under the nail. Still looks good enough to bite.

"Mom! You see this bird? I learned about these birds in school. They can talk! Hey, bird! Say something! Say 'dumb bird'! Come on . . . 'dumb bird'!"

A flock of children close in from every corner of the store and circle the cage like gerbils to prey. The call of the wild.

"Pretty birdie!"

"Dumb bird!"

"Aye, matey!"

"Hey, bird, look at me!"

"Polly want a cracker?"

"Say 'butt'; say 'butt'!"

There are things that'll make you crazy in here.

Twenty minutes later . . . we're still surrounded. I'm beginning to wonder if these kids have been forgotten or abandoned by their parents. There are twelve of them, by my count, spitting, making faces, and picking noses. Aggie's riffling through her feathers with her beak, tugging and fussing with them, clearly upset.

Seven more fingers poke themselves into our cage. They writhe like mealworms but look sweet as baby carrots. I've waited a long time to sample one of these sugary morsels, and I'm just about to decide which one looks tastiest when a single thought dawns on me.

Don't bite! Escape.

Yes. Of course! I quickly survey the room and make sure the list of requirements is in place.

Open door. *Check.* (Still stink-blazing hot in here.)

No Fritz. *Check.*

Ample distraction. *Check.* (Although, still not sure about that second diversion.)

Unclipped wings. *Quadruple check!*

"Aggie—" I say under my breath so only she can hear.

"Yeah?" she whimpers.

"This is it. I'm busting you out. You ready?"

"Uh, um, I—I guess so. I—I'm not so keen on all these kids—one just said he wanted to squeeze me. I just wanna see Fr—"

"All right." I cut her off. There's no time for dallying. "Then here goes nothing."

And I begin to beat my wings.

CHAPTER 13

African greys are not the largest of birds by any stretch of the imagination. But there is a certain amount of force a bird of my stature can create using only his wings and willpower.

I flap. Feathers fly. A dish of seed overturns and cascades to the floor. I squawk using every ounce of breath in my lungs and can tell by the way the children are screaming that it looks like a gerbil-worthy battle's going on. The puppies, unable to stay silent, join in. The whole shop is in an uproar.

"Hey! Hey! What's going on over here? You kids messing with the birds?" I hear Pete yell.

The screaming continues, but I hear one little

girl say, "No, mister! Honest! That bird just went bonkers! I think he's trying to kill that ugly one!"

I flap harder.

"Gah!" Pete squeals. "Get her out! Get her out! That dang bird's worth a fortune!" He lifts the latch and reaches inside to grab Aggie from where she's cowering at the bottom of the cage.

Out of the corner of my eye, I watch as he carefully sets her on the empty shelf behind him and turns back to figure out what to do with me.

I let go of my perch so I'm half flying, half crashing around the cage. I feel feathers break off, feel the stab of pain in my wing, but I keep on.

"Ack! If he breaks a blood feather, it's gonna look like a murder scene around here! You! Kid! Grab that towel over there!"

The whole pack of children turn and run down the aisle to grab towels from a stack. As they do, I see Aggie quietly climb down the shelf and slip herself under the low overhang at the bottom and begin to walk toward the door, half-hidden in shadow.

Parents begin grabbing their offspring, yanking

arms, giving stern lectures. Pete, towel in hand, is looking to grab me.

I continue my campaign until I feel the weight of the terry cloth thrown over me. The trap of Pete's hands snaps shut. Blind now, in thick darkness, I manage by sense.

I feel Pete ease me out of the cage.

I hear the children cheer. I know soon attention will be turned to the other bird. To Aggie.

Five seconds. Ten. Then a glimmer of light.

The towel moves an inch off my head, giving me just enough sight and time. My beak finds its way to Pete's hand for another go.

"YAAAAAAAAAH!"

In an instant, I'm thrown through the air, again, but this time I'm ready. My wings, untested in flight but flapping nonetheless, propel me through the shop. Clumsily, yes, painfully, yes, but I'm flying. Kind of.

Maybe more like bumping off things.

I strain my eyes to see where Aggie's gone. People are running, ducking, covering their heads with purses and puppies; gerbils are squealing with glee at the mayhem.

I make a second flight around the store, Pete on my tail feathers, yelling and sucking his bit finger. As I round the front of the store, I have just enough time to see Aggie's red-feathered end waddle out onto the slushy sidewalk.

Out! Free! I can barely keep myself from following her, but I stick to the plan. First, a diversion big enough for every person, animal, and Pete in the store to forget about me, just as they've done with Aggie.

In seconds I see it.

I thrash toward a long lineup of small plastic aquariums on a top shelf, away from curious fingers. I take aim and come in for a landing, flinging myself headfirst down the line. The plastic boxes topple to the floor and crash, splitting open and emptying their contents.

Twenty-four aquariums clatter. Twenty-four tarantulas scatter.

The noise is deafening.

Grown men are weeping.

Women have climbed the shelving, leaving their children behind to fight off the hairy swarm alone, using broom, dustpan, and the odd can of kitty food as a missile. Paralyzed, Pete takes in the sight of every last crawling escapee as the sky itself falls in on us.

I look to the door.

It's open.

I rocket off the shelf, tasting liberty at last.

Thirty feet.

Twenty.

I'm plummeting.

Ten.

A figure steps into the door frame and begins to sweep the door shut as I'm five feet from freedom. I accelerate. Faster. Faster . . .

Wham!

I'm too late.

I crash into the door and tumble to the floor.

My head is spinning. My eyes are spinning. The room is spinning.

When it stops, I look up to see a face looming

over me. The face of my prison guard, defender of doorways, crusher of dreams.

Cupped between its hands is my sister, still and serene.

I should've known.

It's Fritz.

Stopped by a Fritz on a Snowy Morning[1]

He looks at me with eyes aglow,
His lashes trimmed with fallen snow,
And smile rolled out from ear to ear;
My heart knows all it needs to know.

For Aggie, though, it isn't clear
She'll be without her brother near.
She didn't think that Fritz would take
Just one of us away from here.

I watch them leave, and in their wake,
The heavy-laden storm clouds quake
And loose a bitter howl with me—
To wait so long was my mistake.

My heart's a ruined cavity
And what remains: the cold debris[2]
Of plans I had that weren't to be,
Of plans I had that weren't to be.

---

1. A poem with hints of Frost—Robert Frost. Inspired by his poem
    "Stopping by Woods on a Snowy Evening" (minus the trees).

2. debris (duh-*bree*): what's left after something is smashed into a
    million pieces.

CHAPTER 14

*I*t was a Saturday. Fritz wasn't supposed to be there. My plan should have worked. It *almost* worked. And yet.

Just that morning he'd shoveled a driveway, giving him the last few dollars he needed to buy Aggie, bungle our escape, and take her away. Take her he did.

Again.

And the rest is history.

"I'm not good at good-byes either. Knew it would be hard." Porky sniffs and wipes his nose with an apple peel. "Lentil and Bean, they were good boys, they were. But they're in a better place."

Aggie isn't the only one who's left the shop this week. Porky's twins Lentil and Bean were adopted, and when Bio-Scents boarded up shop, the resulting fresh air turned every day into a Saturday. Pete sold twelve hedgehogs just yesterday.

The day's chaos has dulled and died. Streetlamps spill into the shop. Light glances over shelves and cages, bouncing off the glass aquariums and throwing ripples on the ceiling. Outside, the empty moon has poured its light somewhere else, and the snow, tracing dusty fingers over parked cars left abandoned, lifts and swirls out into the dark. The street is lonely tonight.

Porky lies on his back, staring at the bright waves above him. "We keep on keeping on! That's the thing to do, Alastair," he says.

Fritz took our massive old cage with him. Inside my new, tighter quarters, I turn my back to Porky's case, hoping he'll get the hint. He doesn't.

"We need to celebrate their good fortune! I'll bet my boys are living on a farm as we speak! With all our pig relations! We remember—we always remember—but we can't live in the past, old buddy.

We keep on keepin' on! Maybe take up a hobby."

Nonsense. All of it. I feel Aggie's absence in every inch of my body, every feather.

Behind the register, Pete's Key West poster glows under the streetlamp, and the shadows of a thousand tiny snowflakes float there, on the blue of the sky, the sea. I find myself imagining they're slips of poetry I've shredded. I pick out the tallest palm and try to picture Aggie on the furthermost leaf, chewing blocks and decorating a frond here and there with her finished artwork. We could've rented out a few branches to escaped cockatiels and disgruntled carrier pigeons if we needed. We'd have met future spouses maybe. Had fledglings of our own.

How often had customers complained about the manure smell, and Pete would point to that poster and say, "Welcome to Paradise"?

It seems possible, this paradise.

I snort bitterly.

It wasn't to be.

Porky's still droning on. "Maybe we should start working out. That's a hobby. The hamsters seem to enjoy it." I see him poke a finger into the bulge of his belly. "But if you ask me, I think some extra weight's a good thing for a pig."

The only hobby I'd like to take up is reaching over and biting all the trite words right out of him. Since I can't, I begin my nightly preening but find myself tugging harder than usual at the feathers. One comes out in my beak. I quickly let it fall from the cage.

No need to worry . . .

It's not like that was on purpose. . . .

No feather pickers here!

Across the room, two gerbils get in a fistfight over a sprig of parsley.

"Idiots," grumbles Porky. He shouts over the side of his aquarium. "Knock it off, you vermin! The rabbits need their beauty sleep!" He snorts.

"We were getting it, until you piped up," growls a sleepy Babs.

"Aw, come on, Babs. We're friends, ain't we?" His nose twitches; he looks happy with himself.

"So?" he says to me. "Whadya say? A nightly

game of poker sound good? Hamsters are escape artists—they'll come over as long as we got snacks. We'll just hold your cards up to the glass. We can play for veggies."

"Whatever," I say just to shut him up.

"Great! I'll get Boris over there to join in—guy turns up everywhere. I hear he's part blind, you know. We could make a killing!"

Porky retreats to his sleeping corner, turns a few times, and flops down with a huff. "G'night there, Alastair."

I ignore him and retreat to my feather fluffing, but Porky pipes up again.

"It really is going to be all right there, buddy. Pig's honor!"

I've had it.

"You're not a pig!" I snap, and Porky's eyes get big. "Haven't you listened to Fritz's stupid Latin lessons? *Cavia porcellus. That's* what you are. No relation to potbellied pigs, boars, or any other swine!"

Porky blinks, a little stunned.

"You're a *rodent.*"

I try to ignore the fact that I've used a loose Latin interpretation with my own genus and species as Porky's big round eyes continue to blink at me in bewilderment. I ignore those, too.

I go back to the spot near my shoulder where I left off preening and find a bald patch. I look to the floor.

Five more feathers litter the linoleum.

One

(an original Alastair creation)

> Lonesome, lonely,
> Me here only,
> Single—wholly—
> Left here. Solely.

CHAPTER 15

The Christmas season over, the shop is quiet again. Pete is back to his ornery self, grumbling about the price of dog food or complaining about fickle children who one day adore newts! newts! newts! and the next day want painted turtles, so he's stuck with forty-two newts that he can't even sell at half off. On top of things, every kid who got a hedgehog for Christmas is trying to return it. No one wants a pet that stays curled in a ball, growls, and tries to impale you.

"Sale on newts and hedgehogs! Half off!" he shouts to every customer walking into the store.

The days pass in a hazy fog. The store opens,

things are sold, and the shop closes, a page ripped from the calendar, ready to repeat it all tomorrow. Fritz continues to work his three-day-a-week shift.

His presence is insufferable.

He seems to avoid me whenever possible, except for his gloating greeting soon as he arrives: "Hey there, Alastair! How's it going? Aggie's getting stronger every day! Don't you worry!"

I'll believe it if I see her.

When I see her.

It's been eighteen days, three hours, twenty-two minutes, and fifty-six seconds since I last did.

I spend the days counting the minutes, throwing food on the floor, frightening unsuspecting customers with ear-shredding squawks, and *preening* (barely fussing with) my feathers. The time I have left I spend trying to bend the cage bars with the power of my mind or hiding under my good wing and hating every scaled, furred, and feathered thing that comes my way.

"Gather round, boys! Zucchini up for grabs tonight!" Porky shouts. Boris whistles, and a few of the hamsters take turns chest bumping and high-fiving.

Ever since Porky's started his veggie poker game, mouths on every side yammer the night away: several hamsters, Boris (no one really knows what kind of animal he is, but I heard some of the rabbits say he climbed out of a storm drain and into a cage because it was easy-eating here in the shop), and Vinny, the lone gerbil next door.

Vinny's been shunned by the family for being a pacifist.

"You in, Alastair?" a hesitant Porky asks. "Looks like you got a piece of cucumber there with my name on it." He's kindly been trying to gloss over my outburst these last few weeks.

"I'm in, fellassssss," interjects a voice from the other end of the shop. "Come on over. I'll sssssserve sssssssupper."

"Aw, shut it, Lucifer," shouts Porky.

"Yeah, beat it!" says one of the hamsters.

Vinny shudders. "It's so terribly disturbing. Boa constrictors are just so, so—violent."

"Not in the mood," I manage to grumble between rummaging through my chest feathers. There's rearranging that needs to be done. My plumage lately is, well, a mess.

"Yeah, sure. No problem," Porky says. Then he grins. "Your loss!" he shouts, and begins passing out the cards the hamsters managed to pinch from the front counter.

I watch them. These animals with their late-night poker games, a rabbit beauty shop complete with pet shop gossip, last week's Hamster Olympics (which was really just the hamsters taking turns on their wheel and timing one another until they passed out or got off to get a snack). Everyone's too comfortable, too happy here.

"This is the life, ain't it, boys?" asks Porky after they've gone a few rounds. He's won a few hands, and he's knee-high in zucchini, which isn't saying much since his knees are about a centimeter off the ground.

"Sure is, Porky!"

"You said it!"

"A night out with the boys and good eats—I never had it so good!" sings Boris. "You shoulda seen the garbage I had to eat afore this! Real-life garbage, I tell yeh! If I died today, I'd be a happy ra—bugger!"

Porky eyes him up and down. "Where'd you come from again?"

Boris squints harder at his cards. "Oh, no place special," he says. "But this—this is paradise."

I couldn't agree less.

"You got a chance, Harriet."

Later that night, after the poker players have drifted off to sleep, the moon creeps into that tiny patch of sky, a giant glowing fishbowl. The poker game ended hours ago when Porky lost all his zucchini to Boris, who moonlights as a card shark. Turns out he's a rat.

You should never underestimate the new guy.

I've been up the whole time. Without Aggie's snores to drown things out, I've heard the puppies dare one another to sniff and lick some unknown substance they've found in their pen, the gerbils planning a coup, and Lucifer singing in his sleep: "Ssssssuch deliciousssss little tidbitsssss—hamstersssss—ooh!—gerbilssssss—ah!—mousessssss—mmm. Fat guinea pigsssss and froggiessssss, too. Ratsesssss, oh my, my, my."

The rabbits are up feeding their brood for the fifth time tonight.

"I don't know," says Harriet. "I lost another patch of fur on my rump. I'm looking especially unsightly these days. These kids are gonna be the death of me!" She kicks at a pair of bunnies who've started a wrestling match mid-meal. Once they've settled, she needles her bald patch with the tip of her claw. "Think anybody's got a tonic to put on it or somethin'?"

Babs looks up from licking her paws. "I think Rita's got something—remember how she lost all that hair last year? She put something on it, and it came back all curly."

"Oh yeeeeah!" says Harriet. "Oh, but Rita's got some beef with me these days. I think she's trying to turn a few of the other girls against me."

"Well, you did nip her ear the last time a human was looking to buy."

"But she was acting all cute and sweet! You know Rita ain't cute and sweet. Besides, it was a nice little girl with braids that was looking, and I always said I'd like to be the pet of a nice little girl with braids."

"You never said that!" says one of the other rabbits, butting in.

"Well, maybe not—but that doesn't mean it ain't true!" Harriet yells back.

Vi, the quietest one of the bunch, the one with crossed eyes that always seem to turn off potential buyers, sighs. "I'd take just about anybody."

Babs reaches over and gives her a reassuring pat. "We know, Vi. Don't you worry, hon. You're far from the last one in this shop that'll get adopted. Look at that parrot over there. The day he gets adopted is the day Old Nell keels over."

Old Nell: the shop's oldest living resident and Pete's first pet. "A forty-year-old tortoise in the prime of her life!" Pete loves to tell inquiring customers. It's common knowledge that Pete keeps her here to remind all the wallets and pocketbooks walking into the store what a sound investment they'd be making in buying a pet. He conveniently neglects to mention that most of us have the longevity of a pair of socks. Old Nell, however—the rabbits think she'll live forever.

The girls giggle. "Oh, Babs," says Harriet. "You're so bad!"

"What?" says Babs. "It's true."

"'Course it's true," says Harriet, still giggling. "But that's just mean!"

"See if I care," says Babs. "Been hoity-toity from the beginning. Don't you see the way he's always primping—"

"But we primp, Babs!"

Babs rolls her eyes. "Sure, we primp, Harriet. But he primps so much lately he's torn out his feathers! Look at him! He'll be as naked as a newt soon! With a beak!" They break out in a fresh rash of giggles.

My face is in shadow. They can't see that I'm awake and listening to their every word.

"It's not even that," Babs continues. "Listen, Porky McPorkster and all his fuzzball friends may drive us crazy, but at least they got the decency to talk to us. That parrot thinks he's too good. Only ever wanted to talk to his own kind—that sister of his. He's always brushing Porky off. Barely said boo to me all them times I was in the Infirmary." She sniffs and raises her nose into the air. "Thinks he's *la-di-da*, that one."

"He does cost a thousand dollars," Vi whispers to Harriet. "We cost twenty bucks."

Babs gives her a dirty look. "That may be," she says. "But *five* dollars would be too much to spend on a bird like that. He's a snob. He's always trying to bite anything that walks by. He's . . . he's a *feather picker*!"

I wince.

This time they cackle so loudly they wake the puppies, and soon the whole store strikes up its orchestra of hisses, screeches, squawks, and thumps. Through the noise I make out one last comment from Babs.

"I don't even know what that sister of his ever saw in him."

It's hard to argue with her.

She sort of has a point.

These days—the morning, noon, and evening bustle; the grating noise; the loneliness in a place quivering with humans and animals alike—these things take a lot out of a guy, but the nights . . .

Sometimes the nights take more than you'd expect.

Eulogy for Melman Number Three

You went belly-up sometime during the night.
No one noticed your last gulp,
except for maybe your goldfish kin
who, eyes ever-open, see the whole
world, both awake and asleep, with that
unblinking gape and vacant stare.

Did any one eye shed a tear as you went?

You went belly-up, and though
I knew you no better than
Melman number one or two, I felt an
unexpected diminishment at your
loss—as if some last breath in
you was taken from me, too.

Does the chest sink a bit at every small passing?

You went belly-up, and though there was
no priest, no headstone,
no final word to mark your dying,
I want you to know that in

the moments of your last
walk to the porcelain grave,[1]
there fell such a silence—
over bird, cat, dog, mouse, and man—
that all of
heaven
seemed to wait

in expectation of your soul.

---

1. porcelain grave: the toilet.

Medical Log, January 25

- Age: 12 years 6 months
- Weight: 122.2 lbs
- Height: 53 in
- Current status: Okay, I guess—
  except for that toenail

It was one year ago today that Grandpa died.

It seems like it was yesterday.

We went to the cemetery today, me, Mom, and Fiona. It was cold and windy. It was one of those winds that comes right up the bottom of your coat, finds every hole in your pockets, and freezes your spleen. We didn't stay too long because it started raining, but we left some stuff for Grandpa.

Mom brought roses.

Fiona propped up a small velvet picture of Elvis against his gravestone. Grandpa loved Elvis.

I couldn't think of what to bring. At first I thought

I'd bring my report card, so he could see it, but I got one B, and I didn't want him seeing that. Then I thought I might bring a picture of Aggie to show him, until I remembered how he always said he had a terrible fear of birds after one ran off with his hairpiece. He said it pecked him for good measure as it left. *Never trusted a bird since,* Grandpa always said. I ended up not bringing anything.

When Mom and Fiona ran back to the car to get out of the rain, I stayed for a second longer just to tell Grandpa how much I missed him and how sorry I was. Then I reached inside my pockets because my hands were starting to get frostbite, and my fingers wrapped around some of my medical flash cards. I like to keep them on hand if I'm on the bus, or just whenever.

Grandpa used to sit at the kitchen table with me and test me. Almost every night, right after dinner, just the two of us. I remembered one night he pretended to fall out of his chair in shock that I knew the definition of "zygomycosis." I told him I had a book with that word in the title; it would've been kind of hard not to know. He laughed so hard tears ran down his face. Then he told me I must get my smarts from my grandmother's side, because he couldn't even remember how many toes he had. (He'd lost a few in an unfortunate encounter with a snapping turtle.)

So, when my hand wrapped itself around those cards today, I knew what to do. I found a rock to keep them from blowing away and left a stack of them there. Maybe Grandpa will see them.

And maybe now he'll know the definition of "zygomycosis" too.

Signed: Fritz Feldman, MD

PS As I was trying to think what to write tonight, I caught myself staring at my "rara avis" poster. (Alastair ripped up the last one, so I got a new one for my room.) I realized I never actually looked up the rest of what it meant. So I did.

Amicus verus est rara avis: A true friend is a rare bird.

My dear Everett,

I'm happy to report I've kicked that pesky flu to the curb. It took its sweet time, but I'm fit as a fiddle! I barely left the house except for a few doctor appointments since the new year!

Got me out of the trip, though.

Henry went and bought me an airplane ticket to come visit him and the family in Florida after the holidays. Said he had a big project at work and they couldn't come here for Christmas like their usual.

I'll give you one guess as to what I thought about that.

Persnickety as a pig in a tutu?

Exactly what I was thinking.

Not visiting is one thing. But that boy knows how I feel about airplanes. A few hunks of metal held together by spit and glue have no business shooting me halfway around the world. And let's not forget the last time. Lost in the terminal for an hour before he found me.

I thought I'd have to give him some cockamamie excuse to get out of it, like moths ate my luggage or some such nonsense, but in the end, I caught the flu. And good thing I did, because I have news.

I bought a bird.

Now don't go getting your knickers in knots; one more pet won't do me in!

Here's how it happened:

I couldn't sleep one night, so I decided to hop in the old car for some cough medicine. Even the Thrift Mart was closed by that hour, but as I passed the pet shop, I noticed a light on and figured I'd stop.

Peter looked less than pleased when I rapped on his door, said he was busy fixing his books.

And I decided right then. I paid him no mind, told him I'd come for my bird, and I pointed to the one. He perked up after that. We agreed on a fair price (the poor thing was losing its feathers, so I got the scratch-and-dent special), and I ran on home, got my money, and ran right back to make my purchase.

Your panties are in a pinch right now, I can tell, so I'll tell you what I told Henry.

Parrots make fine companions.

A bird will keep me busy so I'm not calling our son to remind him to take his vitamin C every chance I get.

I always said a person should leave no good deed left undone. I'm taking my own advice. The bird's bedraggled. He needs me.

You only live once. I'm old. Why shouldn't I own a parrot if I want one? Would you deny an old lady a bit of fun?

If anyone's that concerned, I'll teach the thing to call me an ambulance.

All my love,
Your healthy, charitable, parrot-owning wife

PART III

The Great Plopky

—OR—

Alastair's Adventures in Bertie-Land

CHAPTER 16

You can always tell the ones who are buying.

It's never the thin-lipped parents, pulled through the store by their sticky-fingered brood. They've come to fill an hour, not a cage.

It's not the pin-striped couples, either. They come with romantic notions about frizzy poodle pups or sprightly spaniels. They'll leave to buy an easygoing plant.

You can tell the ones who are buying.

It's the eagle-eyed kid with a sack filled with pennies. He trades it in for another one full of goldfish.

It's the terrorized homeowner with a yard full of

squirrels. He'll leave with a squirrel-hunting cat.

It's the misty-eyed lady, empty nested, all alone. She leaves with a parrot and a heart full of hope.

"We're home, Tiger! We're home, Humpty! Yoo-hoo! Look who I've brought with me!"

She took me from the pet shop in the middle of a cold, drizzly night. Fritz was nowhere in sight. Pete was deliriously happy.

I somehow lost fourteen feathers on an eight-minute ride here.

I'm devastated. I'm like a gerbil expecting a massacre—and getting a slumber party.

I'm one of those robins who thinks he's flying into clear blue sky—then crashes into the shop window.

I'm like the kid who thinks his dad's gonna call, only to realize he isn't.

Me? I'm the guy who thought he was going to rescue his sister and now has no earthly idea where to begin.

She paid using small bills—ones, fives, a few tens—her rainy-day stash, as she called it, kept in her hose drawer. "I'm a little embarrassed to be flaunting my undergarments here," she said, "but I couldn't find any envelopes or rubber bands to save my life!" She pulled out a pair of roomy stockings stuffed to the hilt with bills and knotted at the top. Two lumpy legs dangled from her grasp and twitched like dying fish as she drew bill after bill from their open mouths, smoothed them out on the counter, and for an hour kept a running count. In the end, there was a thousand in each leg: a thousand for me, and a thousand for a cage and the various supplies Pete managed to wheedle her into buying.

Fun fact: My life is worth the same as eighty pounds of iron bars, a bag of pellets, and a plastic parrot scratcher.

"Yoo-hoo! Ti-ger! Where'd you slink off to? Don't you want to come meet your new brother?"

Bertie's apartment is a second-floor walk-up on a tree-lined street. Bertie takes me through its rooms, pointing out her bedroom (roughly the size of a closet), the parlor, and the kitchen, furnished with a sink, stove, refrigerator, and small table, draped in a lace tablecloth. A tree of sorts sits at the table's center, balancing four fat red mugs on four limbs.

Everywhere you look, flowers bloom: bouquets in pictures hung slightly askew, petunias climbing the curtains, busy geranium wallpaper. About twenty pillows in just as many floral prints fatten the sofa, while crocheted afghans explode in colorful rainbows along the back of it and drape themselves over every stuffed chair and ottoman in sight.

Bertie rests a hand on her hip and frowns. "Well, I'll bet that rascal is off sleeping somewhere. I guess you'll have to meet him in the morning."

She points to the fishbowl, where a bulgy-eyed goldfish appears to hover in the middle, fins barely twitching. His mouth is a silent O. "That right there is Humpty Dumpty. My Everett bought him for me twenty-two years ago when I retired from teaching—isn't that amazing?" She stops to sprinkle food in the bowl, but the fish makes no effort to reach it. After twenty-two years, I suspect nearly all the life's been wrung out of him.

"Everett said he was just the right pet for an apartment of our size. I told him I wanted a pony. But I wouldn't give you up, Humpty," she tells the fish, tapping on the glass. The goldfish doesn't blink. "Humpty kept me company when Everett was out delivering mail all day. My Everett was a mailman, you know."

Bertie begins to move about a dozen plants from a corner in the parlor. "Your house is being delivered tomorrow," she calls over to me. When she finishes, she brushes a few flecks of dirt from her hands. "There! *Voilà!* There's a big enough space for the cage after all!"

Just then an enormous orange cat saunters into the room. He walks on tiptoe, baby-pink nose held uncommonly high.

"Why, there you are, you darned cat!" exclaims Bertie. She scoops up the hissing ball of fur and comes hobbling over to me, the cat dangling in her outstretched arms.

"See! This here is Mr. Tiger. He's—well, he's none too friendly, but we love him anyway."

"Eat fur, bird," Tiger snarls.

I snap my beak at him.

"Isn't that sweet," Bertie coos. "You two are making friends already."

Anxious and sour, I'm settled in my cage a few days later, taking stock of my feathers, while Bertie's out getting her hair curled.

"My, my, aren't you a lucky bird?"

Tiger oozes past my cage, back and forth, rubbing his side against the bars. He smiles wide and shows off a row of pointy teeth. It's not a nice smile. More menace than mushiness, I'd say. He's bent out of shape because Bertie's given me a heap of toys from his personal hoard.

"Whatcha got there?" he asks. "Is that—is that *my* stuffed mouse?" He rakes a paw against the bars and his claws *chink, chink, chink* on the iron. "What's a wittle bird like you need a mouse for, huh?"

"That yours?" I ask, pointing to the toy at the bottom of my cage. "Funny. Haven't seen you playing with any toys."

"I don't play with toys," Tiger snarls. "I *own* them."

I'm not in the mood.

I'm tired and cranky, and it's greatly increased since I got here.

The last few nights, sometimes twice nightly, Tiger's parked his rump next to the fire-escape window and yowled until Bertie's stumbled blindly from her bed to let him out.

Now, were it simply the call of nature, that would be one thing. But what I thought was a nuisance, a simple case of nighttime overactive bladder, I've come to realize is all about one thing:

Power.

Does Tiger find the kitty lavatory once he's out there? Does he prowl at least, maybe hunt around like any self-respecting cat? Nope. He seats himself two inches from where he just sat . . . and licks his paws.

He. Licks. His. Paws.

You can understand my current appetite for violence.

Tiger stops stalking, and his eyes become slits. "Is . . . that . . . *my* . . . stuffed mouse?" he asks again.

I turn my voice to syrup. "Well now, let me see," I say, climbing down the bars of the cage and hopping to the bottom. "No—no, I do believe this is *my* mouse!" I snatch it in my beak and nearly spit it out. It bears a certain tuna fish aroma.

The willpower of an African grey, however, is steel. I grip the toy harder and pretend to play with the putrid little thing. "Yup—definitely mine," I mumble through its matted fur.

"*Is it?*" Tiger's voice is eerily close to the fine whine of a rabbit. He thinks I can't see it, but he quivers with fury. My eyes are pinned on him. I could see a mouse whisker in his intestine if I wanted to.

"You know," he says, "the last little critter that tried to play with Tiger's toys—now let me see, it was a kitten, wasn't it, a little kitten ol' Bertie thought she'd pet-sit—well, he left. Minus an eye."

"Oh?"

"I can't promise I'll be that easy on a bird."

I smile. "Not to worry," I say. "I won't be staying long."

(What. You thought I wouldn't escape? I will as soon as I chew through these bars. Steel, however, is remarkably solid. It could be a while.)

Tiger raises an eyebrow and freezes mid-clink.

"This whole situation," I continue, "it's temporary. But until then . . ." I dangle the toy within his reach. "It's *my* mouse."

We are locked eye to eye. Seconds tick. Bird and cat. Cat and bird. Nature at its best.

Finally:

"I think not!" Tiger screeches, and, like lightning, a paw flashes out and makes a swipe for the mouse. A single claw comes within millimeters of grazing my chest.

I'm of course ready for it.

The cat may or may not have a deep puncture wound right around the wrist area.

CHAPTER 17

Forty-four days, three hours, twenty-two minutes, eleven seconds.

Fifty days, seven hours, twenty-four minutes, forty-six seconds.

Fifty-five days, six hours, thirty-eight minutes, sixteen seconds.

Since I last saw my sister.

You get locked in a cage for a few weeks with nothing else to do but think about that stubborn pain in your wing, your failed escape plans, and Aggie's sweetly crooked smile, and you get the lay of the land pretty quick.

Let me put this in terms of poetry:

Bertie's your basic sonnet: structured, predictable rhyme scheme, somewhat boring, if you ask me.

Then there's Tiger. A bad free-verse poem. No rhyme or reason, a bit bloated, sloppy, lazy, and painfully self-important.

Humpty Dumpty—he's more of a eulogy. I'm expecting him to go belly-up any moment.

As for me, I suppose if I had to compare myself to something, the closest thing would be a limerick. A bit of a joke. I won't mention the state of my feathers. The bald spots? Probably an allergy.

I've gone from fledgling to plaything (people like to throw their playthings) to prisoner and pet-shop special, then sold off to the only bidder: a little old lady who smells of talcum powder and has an affinity for talking. Behold:

A Limerick

There once was a parrot named Al,
Who had neither sister nor pal.
One day he was bought
(Which steamed him a lot)
By a rabidly gabby old gal.

* * *

"Janet told me last week that pears were on sale down at the farmer's market. Ten cents a pound, Delores told her! I didn't believe her—oh no I didn't. 'Janet,' I says. 'Janet, Delores is blind as a bat. . . .'

"Would you believe they found a paper clip in Alice Stevens's fruit cup at the home? A paper clip right there in the peaches! Nearly choked on it, poor dear!"

Bertie's been on a roll this morning. She's taken two breaths in three hours.

"Guess who signed me up to make a casserole for the potluck supper at church next month? Wait'll I tell Henry. Everyone's talking about how they can't wait to try my tuna noodle!" Bertie frowns. "Delores. She knows I'm no good at casseroles."

Henry is Bertie's only child. She speaks with him every chatty Saturday unless his girls have a baseball game or he's working. When she hangs up, it's the only time Bertie gets quiet. Sometimes she'll lower herself next to the bed, bruising her knees and getting a crick in her neck, as she bows her head and whispers into the mattress. "Casting my cares on the good Lord" is what she calls it.

I'm not sure who this good Lord is, but he must have the patience of a saint.

This week I've heard of nothing but last month's potluck supper in the church basement and how Joan Merton mistakenly used salt instead of sugar in her strawberry-rhubarb pie, and how Reverend Hopkins was the first *to take a big ol' bite and oh! How he did holler!*

"Poor Joan," she says, in today's retelling. "Thought she was doing herself a favor by putting her salt and sugar in those fancy canisters."

Tiger, who's been sitting on the counter all this time licking his paws, suddenly gets up and jumps to the floor, knocking over a box fat with recipe cards.

They scatter over the floor like flower petals.

"Tiger!" scolds Bertie. "You naughty cat! Bad kitty!" Tiger doesn't bother to look over his shoulder as he saunters out of the room. Bertie kneels down heavily and begins scooping up the loose cards. "You know," she says, "I was a prize-pie winner myself."

After a good deal of searching, Bertie unearths a weathered recipe card and holds it high overhead. "Here she is! My Chocolate Cherry Crumble!"

Cherry? My ears perk up.

"Now just look at *this*!" She plucks a faded piece of fabric off her recipe box and holds it out to me. "The blue ribbon—and look! There's my name on it! First prize," she says softly, and shakes her head. "I was a mean, Bertie, pie-baking machine."

Bowing grandly, she turns her sights on me. "And you! Who are *you*?"

I freeze. She's caught me shredding a feather. I've been doing a little more, uh, *preening* lately.

"Shall I repeat myself?" She straightens, throws back her shoulders, and crows loudly, "I, Bertie Plopky, am a very fine pie baker and an *excellent* dancer!" She coughs. "Just not at hip-hop—threw my back out."

She twirls over to a book lying on the table. "I've been reading this *Parrot Pop Psychology*," Bertie says as she taps the cover. "I'd like to know just who you say *you* are, Alastair. Because I know you're no feather picker—"

At the sound of those words, I drop the feather I'm tearing to bits. I was aware Bertie had been bringing home parrot books from the local library and perusing them, but I had no idea they held such close-kept parrot secrets about feather picking.

Someone's been talking.

Bertie continues. "No, I know a majestic bird such as yourself is no feather picker. But are you the intelligent, talkative bird they say you are?"

I wonder who this *they* is and whether it's the same *they* who've been trafficking parrot secrets.

"Blue!" Bertie shouts. She thrusts the ribbon forward. "Blue! This is the color blue!"

I'm not sure her eyes are as good as she thinks they are.

She picks up a pot holder near the stove. "Blue!" she says again. She points to her dress. "Blue color."

She grabs a mug from the mug tree in the center of the table. "Red!" she exclaims. "Red color! We're gonna start with your colors. Give you an education. Give you some purpose! And then I'm gonna start up my senior social again—you need some friends. That'll stop all that feather messing."

Bertie spends the afternoon assembling like-colored objects into little altars of what she calls red, orange, yellow. . . .

I roll my eyes.

Humans. They think they know so much.

Ultraviolet

That ribbon is not *blue*—
    It's ghost-whale ocean-dust.

That couch, it's not *pink*—
    It's pearl-berry petal-wisp.

The chair is not *brown*—
    Rather, birch-bark brandy-light.

The cat is not *orange*, nor the fish—
    They're ginger-dawn brassy-blossom,
        tangerine penny-butter.

No, the leaf isn't *green*—
    Call it pine-puddle meadow-moss.

Your hair isn't *white*—
    It's called gull-frost, sugar-gloss.

And the sun?
    Moonflower-marmalade,
        or
                lemon-luster lightning rod,
                  sometimes
                        amber-autumn copper-spice.

The mug, you say?

My eyes see rose, and wine, and fire, and blood,
    And all you see is—

          red.

CHAPTER 18

The one perk of what Bertie's calling her "School of Parrot Education and Elocution" isn't the color catechism. It isn't the speech lessons either.

It's the distraction.

March comes in like an untrained puppy and learns how to heel. Snow gives way to gentle showers and shocks of sun. I wake to the whistling of warblers again; orioles and buntings flute from the tall bush that crawls up the side of the building; and the thrushes and sparrows banter in the dust puddles. I didn't notice when so many of their songs seemed to disappear last fall, but now that they've struck up a chord once again, I wonder where they went all this while. . . .

And then I wonder how many things you lose turn up again somewhere down the line. Like a walnut at the bottom of your cage you didn't know was there. I mean, if all these birds can vanish into the snow and pop back up once the wind warms like a full coat of feathers, then maybe I can find a wind of my own. . . .

Maybe those winds take you right where you want to go, and I just need to hitch myself up to one. . . .

I wonder how many feathers you need for that.

Are there layovers?

Got to get to Pete's to find Fritz to get to Aggie.

Then there's the Key West palm . . .

And then Bertie will say something like, "Want an apple? Alastair! Say 'apple'!"

And I'll think, *Eh, sure. Haven't had a bite to eat in six minutes. Why not?* "Apple." At which point Bertie melts into a puddle, crooning and praising, and slides over the apple goods.

I know, I know. I've had issues with distraction. But let's face it. I'm not getting anywhere with a search-and-rescue plan for my sister. I'll take Bertie's talking lessons if it means I don't have to think about how much I miss Aggie. Anything not to count the hours, the minutes, the seconds. (Ninety-eight days, six hours, thirty-five minutes, nineteen seconds, by the way.)

We begin with simple words. Easy things to wrap my beak around. Bertie's not a bad teacher, though I would've preferred something a little more gourmet. But there are benefits to small talk. Instead of grappling with something like *My, what a brilliant winged being of high moral character*, I can focus on *Good bird*.

Everyone's gotta start somewhere.

I'm picking up other things too. Sounds mostly. I do a mean fire alarm, garbage truck, and oven timer. (In other news, Bertie has ruined seven Bundts, two coffee cakes, and a tuna noodle casserole.)

I can make Bertie come running to the phone every time I do *that* sound, which can be pretty entertaining, and I can laugh just like Letizia Tortelloni, whose television show Bertie never misses. *Welcome to my kitchen! Take a seat. I feed you. Ha! Ha! Ha!* Perfetto!

But like a scrap of sunshine through this mess of clouds comes my newest ability:

I can meow.

It has given me inspiration.

Ways to Mess with a Cat's Mind:
- Bark and/or growl (useful noises picked up from the dogs next door). This scares the hairballs out of cats.
- Wait for catnaps to squawk loudest. Just when Tiger has fallen asleep is good, but when he's barely balancing on the back of the couch—even better. Laugh gaily after the inevitable screech and fall.
- In best Bertie voice, say one of the following when the cat's not looking:

     a. Tiger COULD use a bath.

     b. Tiger! Time to see Dr. Campbell!
- Drop well-chewed food on cat's head when he slinks past (extra points if you can unload a water dish or two). Shout:

     a. Pee-yew! Tiger stinky! or,

     b. Tiger looks sick!

(See previous example for Bertie's responses.)

It's also inspired some new poetry:

Keep a Little Claw from Me

I have found that
cages
that hem one in
can also
keep things
out.

"I know I've got a whole box here somewhere," Bertie
says one evening, her voice muffled and distant.

She's in the closet.

I'm currently sulking in my cage. (So I ate
the flyers she'd just picked up from the printer's!
Shouldn't have been a big deal.)

A winter parka lands on the ottoman, a sleeping
bag on the lamp. A bowling ball rolls under the bureau
and thunks against the wall.

"Here it is!" Bertie drags out a rumpled box and
flips open the top. "Everett likes keeping two of everything, just in case."

She dusts off a stack of books she's hauled out and sneezes. "I asked him once. I said, 'Everett, why on God's green earth do you need two of the same book?'" Bertie deepens her voice. "'One to underline, one a clean copy.' That's what he said! That man."

The rungs of my cage sing out as, one by one, Bertie plops Everett's books on the bottom. I get a whiff of dust, a faint smell of mildew, and the unmistakable scent of paper.

"I don't think Everett would mind donating his books to a good cause," she says as she leaves the room. I hear her set the kettle on the stove, hear her switch on the small television in the kitchen. Letizia Tortelloni's laugh fills the air.

I look down at Bertie's book offering. I count eight in varying sizes and pop my beak inside for a taste: several anthologies, a Whitman reader, and a hardcover collection of Emily Dickinson's poems. At the bottom of the stack sit two Norton anthologies. They look new, never touched.

Had they been anything else, I could've passed.

But *poetry*.

Haven't had a bite since my days in the back room. How did she know?

I sigh. I never was one for self-control.

Ha! Ha! Ha! laughs Letizia Tortelloni on the television.

Don't mind if I do.

It's remarkable what a serving of Shakespeare can do for the mood.

But later, after poems have gone stale and distractions have disappeared into the night—it all comes screaming back.

Aggie's face blurs in my mind. Did she have that one stubborn feather on the left side of her face or the right? Were there three feathers that stuck up in back, or was it four? What did her eyes look like when she smiled? I forget. How could I *forget*?

It's like Aggie's face is in the clouds—but the clouds are a little too wispy, and the wind's a little too strong. . . .

Excuse me, I have feathers to fluff.

Medical Log, April 1

- Age: 12 years and some days
- Weight: ?
- Height: ?
- Current status: Vision problems? Memory loss/dementia?

An old man walked into the shop today while I was sorting the canned cat food. I saw him out of the corner of my eye—

And dropped a whole case of Mr. Kitty's Kitty Kibble on the floor.

He looked exactly like Grandpa! He had just a little bit of gray hair combed to the side, glasses, and slouchy brown pants like Grandpa used to wear.

I left all the cans of cat food, and I followed him around the shop. He stopped at the fish tanks, then at the puppies, then he went over to the gerbils and shoved his hand inside and got bit, something that would totally happen to Grandpa. He sucked on his hurt finger as he looked through the leather chew toys and the scratching posts. I just kept hiding behind things and watching and filling my eyes up with Grandpa.

But then I realized he didn't walk like Grandpa. Grandpa didn't shuffle, even with a cane.

And his nose was too big.

And he clipped his fingernails too short. Grandpa's were always longer.

And he was too thin, too tall, too creaky, and his earlobes were like quarters.

Grandpa wasn't any of those things. And then I couldn't figure out why I'd thought he looked like Grandpa at all. After a minute I realized he was our old dentist who retired, and I thought it would be nice if I went over to tell him he'd done a really good job on my last filling.

Well, you know that look people give you—like they've seen you and talked to you before, but they don't even know who you are?

Yeah.

It wasn't the only time I got that look today.

The first time was on the bus. My friend James was sitting with someone else, and this older kid sat in the seat next to me, and he started picking at a crusty bump on his knee. Without even thinking, I started saying I thought it looked like actinic keratosis—a patch you can get from too much sun exposure. Well, that's where the look came in.

In the cafeteria, the lunch lady asked me if I wanted peas or carrots, and I asked if they were frozen or canned, because I was trying to watch my sodium intake—the look.

In English, we were supposed to write a nonfiction essay on anything we wanted, and I picked warts because they're really interesting and I'm reading a book called *Feet and Their Ailments*. It was all I could think of. I thought for sure I'd get a really good grade on it, but when my teacher gave it back, there was a big *See me* right at the top. When I asked about it after class, she said my essay sounded more like a romance novel than fact.

Then she said, "For a second there, I thought you loved warts," and I said, "I do!" And then . . . you guessed it.

Mom and Aggie never give me that look. And Grandpa didn't. Dad did a few times, I can remember. And Fiona, well, she's always got all sorts of looks on her face, but it's usually because she's thinking about dances or sea life or mermaid costumes. I really don't like when people give me weird looks— and I get a lot of them. Especially from kids at school. Even my one friend, James. But even a weird look is better than when they don't look at me at all.

I got thinking.

How many other kids get looks like that and don't have anybody to look at them another way? What about kids who get even worse looks—mean ones—or who feel like nobody sees them? What would I do without Mom and Fiona and Aggie?

I've been doing some reading. I'm going to talk to my principal tomorrow, and if she likes it, I'll tell you my idea.

It's a good one.

Signed: **Francis Fitzpatrick Feldman, MD** ← (It's obviously not dementia; I remembered my whole name.)

PS Dad had his secretary send me a real live physician-used stethoscope today! I cannot WAIT to try it out!

PPS And THIS is even better news: Mom got three days off work next month so we can go to . . .

THE NATIONAL MUSEUM OF HEALTH AND MEDICINE IN MARYLAND!

CHAPTER 19

I broke a blood feather last night.

> Blood feather (also known as pin
> feather)—*n.* a developing feather.
> In active growth, a feather will need
> a copious amount of blood to grow
> properly. If broken or cut . . . take cover.

(I ate that definition in the glossary of one of Fritz's parrot pamphlets. I've eaten better.)

It was late, and I was remembering the way Aggie would snore when she got stuffed up, how it sounded like the honeybees that have begun to visit the flower boxes just outside the window, dipping their tongues in the pansies and the few dandelions that found their way there and go unpicked because, as Bertie says, *If that thing's gonna fight so hard to be there, I'm not gonna get in its way. . . .*

That's all, I was just remembering and minding my own feathers' business, and it snapped off. Just snapped right off. Let me describe the experience with haiku:

Blood, oh so much blood
Sprayed over wall, carpet, me—
Gerbils' dream come true.

"That's it!" cries Bertie when she sees me in the morning. "This calls for the professionals! I will not have a depressed bird on my hands!"

Who said anything about being depressed?

Bertie grabs a bucket and fills it with hot water and strong soap. She cracks a few windows before opening my cage to wipe it down.

"Care to step out?" she asks, but I grip my perch harder and look away.

"That's what I thought—depressed."

I'm not depressed. I'm antisocial.

Bertie drops to the carpet to scrub on hands and knees. Her stray pink curler, always overlooked and sort of sad, bounces at the back of her head as she plunges her hands into the soapy water and scrub, scrub, scrubs.

Plunk, splash, scrub, scrub. Plunk, splash, scrub.

She says not one word this whole time.

It must be some sort of record.

Tiger appears in the parlor doorway, sees the mess, and smiles wickedly. He tiptoes around the wet spots in the carpet and over to my cage, a dark gleam in his eye. "Not bad," he says. "Try a few more next time."

Outside, a horn bellows. I peer out the window next to my cage and look down. In the middle of the street, smoke billows out of the open hood of a taxi whose driver is standing above it, scratching his head. A large white box truck idles behind the taxi and blasts its horn. I recognize it instantly.

Pete. His truck from the pet shop. The pet shop

where Fritz works. Fritz who's holding my sister hostage.

Aggie.

There's a plan in there somewhere.

I jump into action.

I just happen to have a dish nearby, and I unload a large helping of kiwi on Tiger's head. He screeches and begins pawing madly at his eyes.

Bertie looks up from her scrubbing. "What's that? What's wrong?"

Tiger's squalling now and barreling through the room like his tail's on fire. "My eyes! My eyes!" he yowls.

"Tiger!" Bertie scrambles to her feet and chases him, arms outstretched, over bed and bureau, chair and china cabinet. The two of them crash into every last stick of furniture in the place. "Tiger! What it is it, baby? Oh my word!"

After an extended struggle, she traps him finally, and within a matter of seconds she's thrown him in his carrier, grabbed her purse, and rushed to my cage to swing the door shut. I panic and make a valiant attempt to stop her, but she manages to trick me. Bertie races out the door, off to the vet, where Tiger will be poked and prodded.

I should be ecstatic. Alastair: 1. Tiger: 0.

But when Bertie sealed my door, she shut out the possibility of escape.

I look down at the street. Pete's still laying on the horn as a tow truck moves into place in front of the smoking taxi.

The apartment door slams closed, and the pictures on the wall rattle. There's a faint creak beside me. I look over to see the door to my cage swing open.

It didn't latch!

Quick as lightning, I climb down the side of my cage. I hit the floor and weigh my options.

The apartment door is stuck tight. But a soft breeze blows through the three windows Bertie cracked to funnel out the soap smell. One opening is slightly wider, and I make a beeline for it.

The window looks into a small courtyard in the center of the apartment building. Clotheslines, strung like spiderwebs over the chasm, shoot from windowsill to windowsill. Bedsheets and blouses of every color wave. A bare patch of dirt carpets the ground below, but above, well, it's not bright blue, but it's sky.

I suck in my breath and squeeze under the window and onto the ledge.

"Who's he, Bob?" asks a pigeon sitting on one of the clotheslines.

"A bird, Frank," answers his astute companion.

I stretch my wings a few times, limbering them up, and step to the edge. I look to the sky . . . followed by the ground.

This is going to have to work.

What was it Fritz always used to say when he played hide-and-seek with my sister?

Three, two, one! Ready or not, Aggie. Here I come.

CHAPTER 20

lap-flap-flap.

FLOOMP.

It's not long after I jump that I realize there's a problem. All is bright and white.

"Where'd he go, Bob?" I hear the first pigeon ask.

"Drawers, Frank," answers the other.

I inch my way up into the light and groan.

I've been eaten by an extra-large pair of cotton underpants pinned to the clothesline.

Figures.

I'm about to give it another go, when a basement door opens, and two barking, snarling Dobermans spill out, spot me instantly, and begin to jump and claw at the brick just a few feet below me.

This is going marvelously.

To risk being swallowed up by another set of drawers or a dog all of a sudden doesn't seem quite worth it, so I decide to walk the length of clothesline. I can scale the side of the building to the top. No problem. I'll fly from the roof, simple as that.

The climb, however, takes longer than expected. It's difficult, treacherous, and almost as annoying as the running commentary I'm forced to listen to.

"What's he doing, Bob?" one pigeon asks.

"Climbing, Frank."

"Why don't he fly, Bob?"

"Can't, Frank."

Can't?

"I can too fly!" I shout. It comes out all slurry— my beak is currently gripping a brick.

"What did he say, Bob?"

"Said he could fly, Frank."

"But we saw him, Bob. He crashed."

"Crashed, Frank."

I feel the color rise in my cheeks, feel the feathers on my head prickle.

"Never knew a bird who couldn't fly, Bob."

"Never knew a one, Frank."

I can't believe what I'm hearing. *I don't have to take this.*

"Beat it!" I shout. "See this beak? Soon as I get up there, I'm gonna make myself a pigeon sandwich!"

"What did he say, Bob?"

"Said something about a sandwich, Frank."

"I'm hungry, Bob."

"I need a sandwich, Frank."

They lift off toward lunch just as I reach the top and clamber over the edge onto the roof.

"And don't come back!" I yell, but they're already out of sight, no doubt scouring the sidewalk in front of the corner deli in hot pursuit of a pastrami on rye.

I run toward the front of the building and the street. I climb another few bricks and pull myself over the lip, and I'm standing on the concrete ledge and looking down on the tree-lined street below. Traffic rushes in both directions. Unhindered.

Pete's truck is gone.

The air rushes out of me. My eyes glaze as cars, taxis, and a bus speed by.

I hear a flap of wings and look over, expecting to see a pair of pigeons. There sits a crow. "What do you want?" I growl.

The crow cocks her head. "Looking for something?"

"Know where that white box truck went?" I ask.

"No," she replies, gazing off past the buildings, the trees.

"Then you're free to leave now."

"But I do know the driver of that truck. Crows always remember a face."

A shot of hope. "You know Pete?" I ask excitedly.

The crow looks wistful. "I know Pete; my mother knew Pete; my mother's mother knew Pete. Pete's face has been handed down five generations—"

"Can you tell me—"

"It was an acorn in his slingshot. My great-great-great-grandfather—fell down dead, he did. Right into a garbage truck—"

"That's nice. Hey, I could use some directions—"

"Not a bad way to go, I guess. Died like he lived. In a pile of garbage."

"Hey!" I shout. The crow's eyes snap back to me. "I need you to tell me how to get to Pete's shop! You know where that is?"

"I do," she replies, sounding a little sore.

"Can you show me?"

"I don't think so."

My patience has shriveled to a raisin. "FOR PETE'S SAKE, WHY NOT?"

She points to my left wing. "That right there," she says. "It's crooked. And look at your feathers. You can't fly."

"I can fly!" I snap, feeling the blood rush to my cheeks again and beat wildly in my ears.

"Prove it."

"Fine." I'll fly out over the roof, just in case. (Wouldn't want any updrafts to catch me and fling me out toward the ocean or anything.)

I feel the crow's piercing gaze on my back as I spread my wings. I take a ragged breath.

Jump.

Flap-flap—

BOOM. CRASH.

Thunder rolls. Lightning flashes. Fat raindrops explode on the rooftop and onto my back as I tumble head over tail and land in the beginnings of a puddle.

"Grow some feathers," the crow says as she takes off toward shelter. "You need 'em."

"It was the lightning!" I shout after her.

I watch the crow become a tiny speck as she soars out over the rooftops. In no time, she blends into the rain and disappears.

Rain drips off my beak, my back. My shoulders ache; my wing aches. My chest aches—right around the heart area.

I trudge back in silence. One step after another.

Another day, another plan, another day, another plan.

There's a long, wet climb down the side of the building, through Bertie's window, and back to the bottom of my cage, where I sit, head resting against the bars, and stare at the door.

Bertie returns an hour later with a sack of groceries and Tiger, who's sporting an enormous cone around his neck.

"Brings out the color of your eyes," I say, finding it hard to put much feeling into it.

"I'm gonna kill you," he growls as he stalks to the bedroom.

Clunks and crashes resound from the other room. Bertie walks back to the doorway of the parlor, holding what looks like a piece of meat on a long fork. "Do you know what today is?" she asks me.

I don't answer.

She peeks around the corner and points the meat toward a silver picture frame on the bureau. The picture is of a much younger, prettier Bertie in a sharp wool suit. A strand of pearls is clasped at her neck, and she holds a small bouquet of violets. Beside her stands a man in uniform, smiling adoringly.

"It's our anniversary today," Bertie says. Her voice grows soft. "Sixty years."

She hoists the piece of meat in her hand. "And look what was on sale down at the market! I don't usually buy roasts—too much food for just me—but sixty years calls for a celebration!"

Still smarting from my failed escape attempt, I'm in about as far from a celebratory mood as you can get.

Bertie returns to the kitchen. I hear her slide out the vegetable drawer, pull a knife from the block. I hear her go about the business of stringing up her roast and sniffling her way through the onions. "I think I'll make some toast to go with that later," she says to herself. "Everett likes rye toast." She pops the roast in the oven and sets the timer. The apartment heats quickly.

Outside, the clouds have rolled back to display a fiery sun. Bertie sets about throwing open more windows, turning on the oscillating fan, and flipping on the TV to an animal documentary I suspect is supposed to be for my own enjoyment. She begins a round of phone calls. I hear about Melly's minestrone and Florence's lawn flamingos for the second time this week. Bertie's dentures clack against each other with every word.

A siren screams past. On the sidewalk, children

shout and splash in puddles as a jump rope slaps the pavement and a metronome of feet make time. Another crow heckles Tiger from the tree just outside the window, and he hisses and claws at his cone. A chorus of tree frogs looks on and laughs gaily.

A fly is caught buzzing at the window. Peas burble on the stove. The oven timer ticks. Plates and forks clank as Bertie sets the table for four. "A place for Alastair, one for Tiger, one for Everett, one for me. It's a special day, after all."

The only silent thing for a square mile is the stupid fish.

All at once the television blares with grunts and the squealing of pigs as they're herded into gates. The narrator's bored voice cuts in. "These hogs who've grown up together will now die together. They've come full circle—destined for culinary greatness."

"Oh dear."

I look over to where Bertie has appeared in the doorway, wiping her hands on an apron.

"Look at that," she says, pointing at the television. "Oh, those poor dears—and here I've made a roast.

It's no different for the cows, I suppose." She looks off to where the roast sits sputtering in the oven. "Well, seems a shame not to admire it, but I suppose we don't have to eat it. We can have a nice supper enjoying the peas and toast and pleasant conversation."

I'm exhausted, angry. The thought of spending an hour as Bertie's sounding board is making the feathers I've got left ache.

"NO!" I shout in Bertie-talk as she sets me at a place at the table.

Bertie blinks, startled at my response. "No? Are you upset about the pigs? It's a shame, I know, but at least they're with their friends," she answers.

Then, without missing a beat, she adds, "That's what you need, Alastair—friends. Now don't you worry; I've got two people signed up for my new senior social tomorrow. I'm calling it Pop-In for Parrots! That'll cheer you right up."

About as much as a pig to the slaughter.

Jabberplopky[1]

'Twas suppig and the loppy crogs
    Did cawk and cargle in the trush.
All grugly were the culinogs,
    And the floxills purflush.

"Behold the Jabberplop, my bird!
    The jaws that beat, the teeth that grate!
Behold the Blubblub Bert absurd,
    The garrulous Bladderskate!"

He snapped his burlsome beak of steel
    To mute this gabwind hag of late—
Then lingered he by the Mugmug tree,
    And stood awhile in wait.

And, at the dinsup time, 'twas fate,
    The Jabberplop, with plate of meat,
Came shobbling through the kitchy gate
    And garbled to its seat!

---

1. Another regurgitation. Followed by a conversation strangely reminiscent
of one I ate in my old Norton. Inspired by Lewis Carroll's "Jabberwocky"
and an excerpt from *Through the Looking Glass*, Chapter VI.

Heave, ho! Heave, ho! Now go and go!
　　The brawgust beak went snipper-snatch!
He left its toast; not so the roast—
　　He chorked that bovine catch.

"And hast thou hushed the Jabberplop?
　　Spread wide your wings, all brainish birds!
O tranquous day! Tralloo! Trallay!"
　　She, openmouthed, lacked words.

[Humpty Dumpty's Explication of Jabberplopky]

"You wanna explain that tripe? Or did your roast snatching mess with your birdbrain?" sneers Tiger, long after my temper tantrum (as Bertie called it).

I call it losing your dang mind.

"Ahem," gurgles Humpty Dumpty.

Tiger gasps. I gasp. Both of us wide-eyed.

"Ahem," Humpty Dumpty repeats. "I can explain all the poems that ever were invented—goldfish happen to be clever poets themselves, you know. Kindly repeat for me the first stanza."

Astonished but able, I comply.

'Twas suppig, and the loppy crogs
    Did cawk and cargle in the trush.
All grugly were the culinogs,
    And the floxills purflush.

"That's enough to begin with," Humpty Dumpty interrupts. "There are plenty of elementary words there. 'Suppig' means four o'clock in the afternoon—the time the great Plopky sits down to *supper* and begins *pigging*. 'Pigging' is simply a fancy word for eating a great amount."

"Uh," says Tiger. "And 'loppy'?"

"Well, 'loppy' means *loud* and *happy*. You see, it's like a portmanteau—there are two meanings packed into one word."

"Well, aren't you smart! What are 'crogs' then?" (Five minutes ago, we'd no idea Humpty could talk, and with a curious British accent at that. Now Tiger's arguing with him like he's done it his whole life.)

"Well, 'crogs' are the *crow* and *tree frogs* just out-side and one discarded *hedgehog*, which I thought none of you had noticed. It appears I was mistaken, however, for it seems Alastair *has* noticed. Beastly things, hedgehogs."

"What about 'cawk' and 'cargle'? Tell me that," snaps Tiger.

"To 'cawk' is to *caw* and *talk*. To 'cargle' is a bit more obtuse. It involves the *caroling* of frogs but also a *gargling* sound, which, in addition to their grumbling, hissing, and clicking, hedgehogs have been known to make whilst abandoned and living under stairwells. It should also be noted that tree frogs tend to *gargle* when they forget to swallow and begin singing with their mouths full of drink. They are a forgetful breed."

"And the 'trush' is the *tree-bush* outside, I suppose?"

"Of course it is."

"But it's also the *trash* can the crow's eating from," Tiger adds, making no attempt to hide his distain.

"Exactly so. Well then, 'grugly' is *grunting* and *ugly* (there's another portmanteau for you). And a 'culinog' is one of those *hogs* on the television—sentenced to their *culinary* fate."

"'Culinary' isn't even a word," Tiger sneers. "How about 'floxills' then? Huh?"

"Yes, well—" Humpty Dumpty sighs. "The 'floxsills' are the flower *boxes* on the window*sills*."

"Fine!" shouts Tiger. "But there's no way you can explain 'purflush'! Oh—oh! You're going to *flush* the kitty down the toilet? Is that it? Flush Tiger down the toilet? I don't even *purr*!"

"It means the flower boxes are *flushed* in *purple* color," Humpty Dumpty says blandly.

Tiger stares, his eyes darting from fish to me and back to Humpty again. He's so completely flustered, an eye twitches.

Finally, he curls his claws into the carpet. "Watch your back, fish," he snarls, then turns to me. "Oh, go choke on a pit."

Humpty winks at me then. And just like that goes back to being *almost* dead.

FROM THE DESK OF
Albertina Plopky

My darling Everett,

Sixty years today, you old dreamboat, you.

Well, let's be honest now.

You'd find, if you were here, that I haven't changed a bit. Mostly. I am still the excellent dancer you married and just as svelte as I ever was.

(Who're you to argue? You always were a little blind.)

But life does look a lot different now, doesn't it? Starting with the one black hole of a change that sucked the air out of everything the day you left in your mail truck and never came back. We argued about the color of your socks that morning. I never imagined I'd be planting tulips on your grave by week's end. Life's full of surprises, isn't it? Good ones, bad ones.

The surprises keep rolling in.

I can say one thing for certain: time sneaks up on you. The days are all sly and quiet. But the years jump out at you and bop you over the head!

Our son.

Henry.

I never did think I'd see him as grown as he is, sure didn't. And my, how he's turned into you, through and through. Henry may not be as quiet as you were (he gets his feistiness from me), but he's certainly a grump when he wants to be, a real stick-in-the-mud. He's a responsible boy, though, works hard, looks out for his mama. You'd be proud of him, Everett. You really would. He sounds just like you too. So much so that my heart's nearly broke by the time I hang up the phone. As if missing him isn't enough, I've got to miss you, too, each time I talk to him. Oh, and he's got two beautiful girls, Everett. I wish you could see Henry with them. He's a wonderful father.

And here's another surprise.

I take no pleasure in admitting it, don't like to own that I'm wrong, but Henry? He was right about the bird.

This whole kit and caboodle isn't turning out how I thought it would.

I guess I thought we'd all get along like peaches and cream. Thought I'd be able to make that sorry bird happy. Well, I'll be darned if it just isn't so! When Alastair isn't making a mess, or sulking, or tearing out his feathers, he's torturing the cat. He looks just dreadful, Everett. Come Thanksgiving, I'll have to hide him, he looks so much like a turkey. Just needs gravy.

He's such a sad thing, honestly. Always fighting me about something. Earlier, it was about locking his cage before I left. Wasn't until I pointed out the window and shouted, "Would you look at that! A cherry tree!" that he got distracted long enough for me to latch the door. Silly thing, really. Out of the blue, I remembered Peter mentioning the bird had a taste for cherries. I don't like fibbing, of course, but in the end, it was all I could do to keep my fingers intact.

Then this evening, I made us a special supper, and oh, that bird! First, he argued with me. Told me *no* just like a toddler! Then, when we sat down to dinner, what did he do? He forked his beak into that piping-hot

roast and chucked it right off the table—like
he was making some kind of statement! I
was none too happy, mind you, but the whole
thing was so astonishing I had to ask myself if
you were up there playing a trick on me.

(You never did get me back for the time
I put whipped cream in your postal cap, did
you?)

Oh, I miss you, Everett. I'll never stop
hating the fact that you're gone. I needed
you in this life. Remember how I called you
strong and silent as a mountain? Remember
how you'd say I was dogged as a dandelion?

It's because I had you. You were my
Everest, my firm ground. A root doesn't hold
without something to hold on to. That was
you. Without you, well, let's just say there's a
little less pluck, a little less fight.

Sometimes, a wee breeze seems enough to
blow me right away.

Who would have thunk it.

Happy sixty years, my love.

Always and forever,
Your Bertie

CHAPTER 21

The unexpected creeps up on you. One moment it's silent in the shadows (or the enigmatic depths of a fishbowl), and the next moment it explodes on the stage, throws you a curveball. You can't predict where lightning will strike—or when a goldfish will explain your poetry with perfect literary criticism.

Life is weird. Unexpected. Surprising. You never know what's around the corner. It could be Fritz stopping you in the shop's doorway.

Or it could be his knee.

And your sister.

* * *

The next day, as Bertie and I push through the tall oak doors of the Shirley River Community Center, my travel cage runs smack-dab into Fritz's kneecap.

I'd know his smell anywhere.

"*Sufferin' sciatica!*" he squeals as he jumps on one foot, holding his knee with one hand and a leash with the other. Aggie, wearing a small harness attached to the leash, flaps her wings, frantically trying to stay perched on Fritz's shoulder.

"Oh, oh my," says Bertie, feeling for her glasses, her brow knitted in concern.

Fritz stops hopping. "Oh, no—this is great!" he says, a large cheesy smile pasted on his face. "I can finally wear that knee brace I bought last year!"

"Oh!" exclaims Bertie. She squints as she reaches out and brushes a few cheese-curl crumbs from his shirt. "Are you sure you're all right, dear?"

"I'm all right!" chirps Fritz. He steps back and raises an eyebrow. "Hey," he says slowly. "Don't I know you? Mrs. Plopky, isn't it?" Fritz bends over and retrieves Bertie's glasses from the tile floor. "It's me, Fritz! From Pete's Pet (and Parrot!) Shack, remember?"

"Oh, Fritz!" Bertie adjusts her glasses. They sit crookedly on the bridge of her nose. She peers at him. "Yes, I do remember you! How are you, dear? And here's your parrot friend! Yes, yes, of course—you're the young man who convinced me to buy my Alastair."

She lifts my cage so it's eye level with Aggie, and my heart explodes a little.

"Leapin' lockjaw," murmurs Fritz. "*There's* your brother, Aggie."

"Alastair!" Aggie squeals.

"You here for this?" Fritz thrusts a flyer in Bertie's face, and she steps back to read it.

"Why that's an old Polka with Pets flyer!"

Fritz nods. "My sister, Fiona, gave it to me. I told her I was interested in making a program for kids and emotional support pets at my school. I was just checking out this senior citizen one for ideas. No one's here yet, though."

"Well, I am," says Bertie. "It's my class."

Fritz's eyes get big. "Then I have a million questions to ask you."

Fritz and Aggie follow us into a small gymnasium draped in sagging crepe paper and a few wilted balloons. A circle of metal folding chairs is convened on the stage.

Bertie sets my cage on its own folding chair and Fritz props Aggie on the chair back. Aggie beams and shivers with excitement. I'm overcome.

"How are you?" Aggie shrieks. "Oh, I've missed you! Oh, look at your feathers! What happened? Mites? Do you love your new family? *Oh Mylanta!* I can't believe you're here!"

Aggie's apparently picked up some Fritz *phraseology*.

While Fritz peppers Bertie with questions, Aggie and I spend a frantic hour trying to catch up over the sound of a work crew installing a new wood floor.

"Bertie bought me the day—"

Bang.

"She's got a hideous cat named—"

Bang.

"Now we can come up with a plan to—"

Bang. Bang. BANG.

* * *

I'm in quite the mood by the time Bertie and I return to the apartment later that day. The elation I felt at seeing my sister has cooled to a temper. Though Fritz convinced Bertie to join him for a burger at a crowded, noisy Burger Den afterward, Aggie and I swapped only snippets of conversation across the booth. That was *before* Fritz buried my cage under his research articles, completely cutting me off from my sister.

Typical.

Worse, I still have absolutely no idea where Aggie is or where she lives.

Bertie deposits me on top of my cage, but I climb down the bars, shove inside, and stalk to the corner, tugging at my feathers as I go.

"Oh dear," says Bertie. "Something's wrong. You're messing with those feathers again."

"You're dang right something's wrong!" I answer. (It comes out more like *SQUAWK*.)

Bertie frowns. "I know you're disappointed those other folks didn't show, but at least we had Fritz and Aggie! The others will be there next time—I'm sure of it." She makes her way to the bedroom. "I think somebody needs some cheering up."

"*NO*," I shout. "*SQUAWKITY SQUAWK. BAD TIGER. SQUAWK.*" Translation: *I don't want cheering up! I'm tired—tired after seeing Aggie today and then watching Fritz take her away again, tired after yesterday's flying failure and this useless wing! And that's not all! Your cat is abominable! I'm tired of him, too! Waking me up four times a night so he can get let out to lick himself—haven't had a good night's sleep in weeks! And yes, I may have picked a feather or two since. So what? Other birds have done so in less distressing circumstances!*

(By the way, retaliation for Tiger has been an aerial assault. I've managed to dump four bowls of food, thirteen dishes of water, and one well-aimed dropping on his head. You take what you can get.)

"And another thing—"

Bertie crashes into the room, wheels around, and strikes a pose. I stop mid-squawk.

Paper fan in hand, feathers wrapped around her neck and trailing behind her, Bertie has a slipper on one foot and a bandage on the other where she stubbed her toe letting Tiger out last night. She shimmies toward the record player, selects an album, and slides the needle in place. A volley of trumpets, snare drums, and the nasal voices of the Andrews Sisters surge into the room. Bertie turns in circles, wiggles, jiggles.

"It's therapeutic, Alastair! Brings out the endorphins!" she shouts over the noise. "Fritz talking about how pets and different things can help people feel better—why, it made me think of the things that make me happy! Like dancing!" She twirls and nearly trips over the ottoman and cracks a hip into the bureau. "You should try it!"

"I'll pass," I squawk.

"Don't sit under the apple tree with anyone else but me, with anyone else but me, with anyone else but meeeeeee . . ." Bertie sings into the television remote, bangs into the lamp, and knocks off its shade. It promptly lands on the cat, who runs off yowling.

I'd tell her that if she'd go ahead and open her eyes, maybe she could see where she was *dancing*, but I'm not sure it matters. She looks—ridiculous. I feel a smile threatening to form but wipe it away.

I'm still mad.

"Come on, shake your tail feathers!" Bertie stops wiggling to look at me and puts her hands on her hips. "No? Not in the mood? Dancing not your thing?"

"Have you noticed my tail feathers lately?" I squawk, showing her my rump. "Yeah, me either. Because they're *gone*." I've uttered nothing remotely close to Bertie language, but Bertie seems to understand.

"Have it your way," she says a little sadly. "Don't know what you said, but it didn't sound good." She turns off the record player and shuffles back to the kitchen. "Maybe another time."

The sound of bowls and dishes being plucked from the cupboard and set on the table echoes through the apartment. Bertie grabs a bag from the refrigerator, and I spy a burst of scarlet.

"We need something to make us all feel better. Maybe some baking therapy'll work," I hear her say to herself. She calls over to me. "I'm going to make something special for dessert! Just you wait! It'll be a surprise!"

Just then Tiger slinks back into the front room and up to my cage. "Surprise!" he says. "It's parrot pie!"

I dump a bowl of birdseed on him.

Bertie looks in at the noise of a million seeds skittering across the floor. "*Again?* Ooh! You two!" She grabs the cat, stomps to the fire escape, plunks him outside, and slams the window. The tip of Tiger's tail gets caught under the frame, and he lets out a spectacular yowl.

Bertie: 1. Tiger: 0.

"Serves you right!" Bertie shouts. "You're in time-out!"

She marches back to my cage. "I'm going to forgive you for that shenanigan," she says, shaking a spoon at me. "Besides. Don't need to put you in time-out, do I? You do it yourself."

Bertie wades through the sea of birdseed toward her bedroom. "Now, I'm going to have my nap before I clean this mess and finish my cherry crumble. Stay in there and behave yourself!" she calls out to me.

At her suggestion I decide to get out and stretch my legs.

This Is Just to Say[1]

I have sampled
the cherries
you abandoned
on the table

the ones
I think you
intended
for a pie

Beg your pardon
they had pits
I left those
in the bowl

---

1. You might have thought this poem was "This Is Just to Say"
   by William Carlos Williams.
   It's not.
   It's only a tribute. Call it "This Is Just to Say" . . . à la Alastair.

Medical Log, April 18

- Age: 12 years 9 months
- Weight: 122.8 lbs
- Height: 53.1 in (I grew!)
- Current status: Flushed, respiration high, contusion on knee (currently braced), AND found a wart on my big toe yesterday (same toe as the ingrown toenail)!

You won't even believe it. Guess who I found today?

Alastair!

A long time ago an old lady came into the shop. I was scared that day. I thought she was going to buy Aggie because she was looking to get a bird for a pet.

Well, it's the same lady who bought Alastair! She's had him the whole time. (I don't know why Pete told me a circus clown bought him.)

Me and Aggie were going to this sort of class for old people and animals today—I thought it was going to be like one of the pet therapy places I've been reading about—and we bumped right into them. It was Mrs. Plopky's class. She was really interested in hearing about all the research I did. I showed her all my articles.

I told her animals can help kids in lots of ways at school. You can use them to help teach lessons because a kid will stay really interested if an animal's your teacher. Animals make you feel good just petting or feeding them, and they can help kids feel happier when they're sad or stressed.

Mrs. Plopky liked hearing about it so much we ended up going out to Burger Den to talk more. She bought me two Big Bear burgers, fries, a milkshake, and a side of Grizzly grits. We talked for two whole hours.

She told me all about having Alastair as a pet. I told her about Aggie.

We talked about our medical conditions. I prescribed a castor oil treatment for her corns.

I told her about James making fun of me last week for taking out another mental health book from the library, and how he told some of the ninth graders on our bus yesterday that I wore nervous system pajamas when he slept over once. (That was years ago, and I loved those pajamas. They were really lifelike—right down to the dendrites.) When the kids laughed, he told them about my Halloween costume too.

"So what if you dressed like a kidney for Halloween?" Mrs. Plopky told me. "I don't think wearing a bedsheet is anything to write home about!"

I had to laugh then because James actually *was* a ghost that year, and my costume *was* pretty amazing. I even figured out how to squirt yellow mustard out of it.

We talked about Grandpa Bud, too. I told Mrs. Plopky how we used to put grape jelly on everything. About how we played checkers and I always beat him. About him quizzing me on my flash cards. I even told her about the medical charts and how Grandpa used to let me take his vital signs and log them just like a real doctor does.

I wanted to tell her the rest of it, but I didn't.

Signed: Dr. F. F. Feldman, MD

CHAPTER 22

So this here's my new bike, Mrs. Plopky!" Fritz said, working the lock and freeing his bicycle from the rack outside the community center. He jangled the bell, a bell as loud and obnoxious as its owner.

"See, it's got a sweet bell, and this basket here in back opens and shuts—and the best part: a perch right up here by the handlebars for Aggie." Sure enough, a wooden perch and small harness were clasped to the bars.

"That is a lovely bicycle!" Bertie exclaimed. "And a perch, too! You've thought of everything."

"I bought it because I just got two paper routes,"

said Fritz. "Every morning at six a.m. I'm delivering news to all the people of Banks and Poplar Streets, and over on the other side of town, on Cherry Tree Lane, that old-folks home—the Prickly Pines? I deliver papers to almost every room. Old people really love their newspaper."

Bertie whooped, and a squirrel fell out of the maple behind her. "Fritz! I live on Poplar! Eighth block. Brick apartment building with all the flower boxes."

"I know just the one!" said Fritz. "That place is good for my blood pressure because I gotta climb four flights of steps. I deliver to twenty-four people in that building."

"Me included," said Bertie. "Apartment 216. One of these days, I'll scoot you inside for a mug of tea."

Fritz frowned. "I don't know. People can be awfully particular about getting their newspaper on time."

"Oh, well." Bertie reached up then to pat her hair and sighed as she found a curler still stuck to her head. "We'll figure out a time. You can bring Aggie. I'm sure that would cheer Alastair right up."

"I will—I promise! Plus, you can help me with my gerontology research," Fritz added.

"Whatever you say, dear."

That was the conversation.

A lesser bird might have thought nothing of it. But let's not forget:

I am not a lesser bird.

Here's the thing. I appreciate Bertie's parrot school. I'm grateful for the poetry. And I was pleasantly surprised at Bertie's reaction to the cherry stealing. (All she said when she found me sitting in my cage looking as guiltless as possible was, "So much for my pie. Did you enjoy them, at least?" To which I squawked, "Maybe." And she said, "At least you cleaned up after yourself.")

It could've gone worse.

But much as I'm beginning to—well, "like" is such a strong word, so—*tolerate* Bertie, there's still this problem of my sister. The problem being: My sister lives with Fritz; she does not live with me. *That* is the ever-loving problem, and one that must be remedied. For good.

In the week since that conversation, a plan's begun to hatch. I've been waking before the sun, earlier each day. Finally, two days ago, I woke early enough to hear the ring of Fritz's bicycle bell.

Of course he rings it at six in the morning.

It breaks into the sleepy quiet, cutting short the twittering of birds and causing dogs in the surrounding yards to bark. I've listened. I've counted minutes, seconds.

By my clock, Fritz spends exactly sixteen minutes, thirty-seven seconds delivering papers to the four floors in our building (and more like nineteen minutes when he drops a bag of newspapers down the stairwell—an amusingly long racket) before he's back on his bicycle, bell sounding all the way down the street at even intervals. (One can only assume he must ring it with each paper he throws.)

Are you thinking what I'm thinking?

Operation Aggie

Step 1. Night before my extrication, prove difficult to cage (try biting, hiding out of reach, et cetera).

242

Bertie will eventually give up and go to bed.

Step 2. Before dawn, emerge from hiding spot and move to space behind window curtain. Wait for Fritz's bike bell to sound below window (approximate time: 6:26 a.m.)

Step 3. Growl. If Tiger's in deep enough sleep, he won't be affected. Plan can continue.

Step 4. Meow.

Step 5. Hidden by the curtain, wait for half-asleep Bertie to "let the cat out" (i.e., open fire escape window).

Step 6. Escape out said window like your tail feathers are on fire.

Step 7. Fly? Float? Flutter? Flop? to ground and hide self in Fritz's bicycle basket.

And Step 8. Let Fritz chauffeur you, unawares, to Aggie.

(From Fritz's to Key West: to be determined at a later date)

It's brilliant, if I do say so myself.

CHAPTER 23

*I*t's been raining for days.

Bertie sighs. "How I melt in the rain. It's the only thing Tiger and I agree about—neither one of us want our curls wet." The forgotten curler at the back of her head looks limper than usual. Dejected even. "Plus, I don't like driving in it. Phooey. Rain."

Phooey is right. A bird can't escape in it either.

But after the fourth day of missing all her appointments, Bertie's decided to brave the weather for the community center and a trip to the corner store for essentials. She's out of oatmeal.

In a splash of rainwater, we rumble up to the two-story, brick Shirley River Community Center.

Bertie sets the car in park, turns the key, and the rusty heap coughs and gives up the ghost in a cloud of exhaust. She pops open an umbrella and grabs a sandwich-board sign from the trunk. POP-IN FOR PARROTS MEETS HERE, the sign says in bright red lettering. And just below, somewhat smaller: A SOCIAL HOUR FOR SENIOR CITIZENS AND THEIR PETS (PARROTS AND PETS NOT REQUIRED). Bertie lugs it over to a puddle-less spot on the sidewalk, sets down her umbrella, and arranges the sign as the rain slaps against her slicker and the plastic kerchief she keeps over her curls.

"We're here!" Bertie says, retrieving my travel cage from the back seat. "Are you ready to meet some new friends? Got a couple new people signed up this week. Fritz and Aggie won't be here, but we'll manage. It's what we're here for. Friends and good feelies."

Fritz has missed Bertie's pop-in the past two weeks, once for a conference on bone spurs, and this time for a destination vacation to the National Museum of Health and Medicine.

Bertie hauls my cage up the steps and through the

oak door, huffing and puffing like the broken bellows of an accordion. The gym is dark when we step inside. Bertie flips a light switch, and nothing happens. She tries another. "Oh poo. The power's out," she says.

It's dreary outside, but the large windows in the gymnasium send in just enough light to see by. Bertie lugs my travel cage up to the stage and sets it on the folding chair next to her. She pulls off her kerchief and slicker, shakes off her umbrella, and sets all three beside her. She folds her hands in her lap and stares at the door.

"Now we wait."

We wait. And wait.

In the dark. In the quiet.

For friends and good feelies that never come.

We return home in silence. Bertie carries my cage up to the apartment and goes back down to gather her groceries. "That step nearly got me this time," she says as she unties the plastic curl-protector from under her chin. She places the dripping umbrella on the radiator and carries a sack of groceries to the kitchen.

"I keep telling Donny downstairs to fix that step.

Donny, I says, I'm gonna take a spill, and it's gonna be all your fault. You're gonna have to come bring me flowers in the hospital, and violets are my favorite."

She pulls a canister of oatmeal from the shopping bag, then unearths a flash of scarlet. My eyes pin themselves to it. Another flash.

On the counter, two large bags of cherries sit gleaming in a pool of lamplight. I tremble.

Bertie turns the radio dial to the wail of a few bluesy horns and sets about her baking. She stays mostly quiet, a stark contrast to the constant drone of the last week. Henry's away on business, Alice and Betty are off on a cruise, and Irma's got a new cell phone she doesn't know how to use. The rain having kept Bertie from trips to the beauty parlor, the post office, even church, her listening audience was down to three: Tiger, the fish, and me.

"Forget dinner," I hear her say to herself. "Weather like this calls for pie. Pie'll cheer anyone up."

The table is set for three.

Rain beats against the window as Bertie shuffles

over with two large pie plates. She's spent the afternoon pitting cherries, rolling out dough and pinching it into pie plates, and slopping a gooey cherry mess in the middle of it. One pie has a crumbly brown top. The other has a blanket of flaky crust. I can make out something written on top of it, but I can't get a taste for the words from my spot at the table.

"I had planned on making a pie for Joan with the last batch, but Joan's doctor says she needs to cut back on the sugar, and anyway, *we* could use the pie, now couldn't we? One prize-winning Chocolate Cherry Crumble, and one *Pie Surprise*, coming right up. Sound good?"

Drat. "Sounds suspicious," I squawk.

"Sounds suspicious," Bertie agrees.

Bertie sets an entire pie in front of me and the other at her place at the table. "Here we are. I gave myself the Chocolate Cherry. Chocolate's not good for birds." Bertie lowers herself into her chair. "Go ahead—dig in."

I look down at the pie in front of me. A flaky

layer of pastry rests on top, with words painstakingly written in tiny flaxseeds.

I am *not* eating it.

Now I get it. It's revenge pie. Bertie's getting me back for eating all her cherries the last time.

Maybe she's followed Joan's recipe and put in the wrong ingredient.

It's full of kitty litter, I know it.

Pie Surprise, my foot.

"Oh, silly me, I forgot the tea," Bertie says. She grabs the kettle and pours a mug for herself and one for the absent Everett, whose picture is propped on the table.

"A slice of pie, dear?" she asks, and serves his picture frame a slab. "My Everett loves this pie. You approve of pie for supper, don't you, Everett?" She waits for an answer. "Good. Me too."

I look down at my pie again. I'm feeling my willpower ebb with each waft of cherry. I can't smell the kitty litter yet, but I'm sure it's there. The words I can't read, but they call to me too.

Probably says something really bad.

A crash of thunder cannonades into the room. I pitch forward, and failing to catch myself, my beak cracks the surface of the piecrust. I straighten and lick the cherry goo from my beak as Bertie looks up, surprise on her face. She quickly realizes I don't want to be ogled right now and lowers her eyes to her own pie.

I'm glad she's being considerate.

I dip my beak in again. I pick around for bits of kitty litter, but it's all sweetness—warm waves and pools and pockets of cherry. The taste is better than the smell. Divine. Sublime. I catch the taste of the flaxseeds and the words. They bump into one another, sorting themselves out. I continue to eat, and a simple poem takes shape in my mouth. It's Bertie's. It's what she's written on the pie.

Roses are red
Violets are blue
Cherries are sweet
And Alastair too.

My beak hits the plate. I look down.
I've eaten the whole pie.

Bertie looks up again. Her face breaks into a sad sort of smile, and she winks at me. "Maybe we should eat pie for dinner more often," she says.

"Maybe we should," I answer.

All right, so she's not so bad after all.

Thirteen Ways of Looking at a Bertie[1]

I
Amid thirty flowered pillows,
All that stirred
Was the mouth of a Bertie.

II
I reckon I should fly
To a palm
With an absence of Berties.

III
Bertie spun like a polka record
And crashed a padded hip into the unoffending bureau.

IV
A husband and wife:
A family.
But a husband and his widowed Bertie?
It changes nothing.

---

1. A Bertie-flavored poem inspired by "Thirteen Ways of Looking at a Blackbird" by Wallace Stevens.

V

I cannot think which I like better,
The prior calm
Or the stillness after,
Bertie's silence before the phone's ring
Or the final click of the receiver.

VI

Raindrops tapped against the fire escape
In melancholy time,
As the age-bent shape of a Bertie
Trotted dismally by
Dusting
Her path with words
And the motes from silver picture frames.

VII

O wise fish, Humpty Dumpty,
Do you sense something deeper?

Does Bertie scatter
More than fish flakes
On the waters of your bowl?

VIII

I have savored Norton's prose,
Relished rich and piquant[2] poems;
But I taste, too,
Bertie's pie
And the simple words she left there.

IX

When Bertie tangoed to the kitchen,
A lot of noise left the room
And a little light.

X

It was just a glimpse of Bertie,
Dancing with the teapot,
That found a bird of stolidity[3]
With a smile of his own.

---

2. piquant: pleasantly strong in taste.

3. stolidity: the quality of remaining always the same and not reacting,
   changing, or showing much emotion or interest. (I ate that exact
   definition from the Oxford Advanced Learner's Dictionary.)

XI

He dropped letters in every mailbox
The county over.
When his heart gave out
On a winding country road,
He left a truck full of bills and unopened birthday cards,
And a Bertie.

XII

The clock is ticking;
Bertie must be talking.

XIII

It was dark in the gymnasium.
The sky broke open
And continued to break.
And there Bertie waited,
Wiping tears from her wrinkles.

FROM THE DESK OF
Albertina Plopky

Dear Everett,

Let me set the record straight.

I did not hit that fire hydrant on the way home from the community center last week, I don't give a fig what Delores says.

But thanks to that meddling old bat, everything's gone topsy-turvy.

Henry decided he was going to make me take a senior citizen driving test. Said he was going to come up here and take my keys if I didn't. You can imagine my reaction.

Your son and I have traded phone calls, written letters. He's been no peach, let me tell you. Started in on me about moving again too. We've been duking it out for what seems like forever over these nasty bits of business; I never thought he'd finally put it on ice, let me have my own way.

Then today I get a letter. Says he's done

pestering me about Florida, about the Pines, about my driver's license. Said he can give me a recipe, but he can't make me cook.

I don't need bifocals to see he's looking out for me, thinks he'll keep me out of trouble. But I see things the way I see them. There's no changing an old bird's mind when it's stuck on a thing. (Plus, I can throw a mean kick to the shin when it's called for.) I got my reasons for wanting to stay cooped up in this old apartment. Henry might not like them, but they're reasons sure. He might find he's got a different pair of eyes when he's on this side of the hill.

I know I'm no spring chicken.

I may not be as spry as I once was.

I may get tired sometimes and have an ulcer that acts up.

Got more chin hairs than I'd like to say.

Getting old is the pits.

But I don't want to be depending on anybody. I've been driving for sixty-five years, and nobody's taking that away from me. It's like taking flight from a bird.

I'll be right as rain here. Surrounded by my pictures and pets. With your old books and window boxes that would hurt too much to leave. The three of us were a family in these rooms. And all those memories can stay whirling in the air, making me smile a million smiles. I'll be smiling here till my dying day.

And that's just fine by me.

Love always,
Bertie

Medical Log, May 19

- Age: 12 years 10 months
- Weight: 122.4 lbs
- Height: Only 53.0 in (I had on two pairs of socks the last time.)
- Current status: Pretty okay, minor cramping in the lower abdominal region (reassess hourly for possible appendicitis diagnosis), ingrown toenail still, wart

Mrs. Plopky was supposed to come for the grand opening of the Pet Pals room at school yesterday. We were both really excited about it.

But she never came.

So this morning, I got up enough courage to knock on her door while I was delivering papers. She seemed really happy to see me and told me it's been raining too hard to drive and that she hasn't been feeling like herself lately. Then she invited me to meet her at the Burger Den after school to make up for it.

She came in a taxi. We got a booth by the window. I told her how Aggie was a hit and how almost everyone in school wanted to come visit her. Kids I don't think I've ever even seen were coming in to pet her and feed her cashews. I told Mrs. Plopky about James and a few of the older kids who said pet therapy was dumb, but she said they were nincompoops and not to pay them any mind.

And there we were, watching the rain and sipping our milkshakes, when out of nowhere, I told her the secret. I don't even know how it came out of my mouth. It just slipped out!

I thought she'd get upset and give me that look people give you when they feel awkward around you now. I thought she'd at least agree that I made a big, huge, awful, horrible mistake. But she didn't. She just looked at me real calm for a long minute. Then she said, "Well isn't *that* just the pits."

At first I thought it was a weird thing to say. I mean, when somebody tells you they let their grandfather die—because they missed the early warning signs they shouldn't have missed because they were all right there in their medical chart, and that maybe they even tried to tell themselves it was nothing and that everything was okay because they were just too scared and couldn't even think of what to do—then saying it's the pits doesn't seem very nice. I thought maybe she didn't really hear me because I was crying, so I said it again. That Grandpa Bud had a stroke right there in front of me, and I didn't do anything. He died. And it was all my fault.

"Is that why you started your Pet Pals?" she asked. And I kinda nodded my head and told her it was partly why—not the whole reason; I wanted to help other kids too.

She stared at me for a few seconds again, like she was thinking. Then she shook her head, reached for my hand, and said that carrying that weight is an awful burden to bear and one I didn't need to. She said it was just the pits that I had been for so long, that it was absolutely not my fault. No kid should bear the burden of a doctor, she said, and any way you look at it, there are times the good Lord calls a person home and there just isn't a thing anyone can do about it. All I could really do was just nod my head and listen.

She said Grandpa would've hated me blaming myself and that living that way wasn't doing anyone any favors. She told me to leave that guilt right there in that Burger Den booth and walk right on out. Then Mrs. Plopky said this:

She said life's a lot like baking a pie. Something as small as salt can screw the whole thing up if it's the wrong ingredient.

"And the past is the past," she started to say. "Don't go ruining your pie because you left any one thing in the oven too long." But then she stopped.

I thought Mrs. Plopky almost sounded like Letizia Tortelloni for a second, and I was hoping she'd explain what she meant a little more. But then she flicked her hand like she was waving something

away and patted my cheek and said she was going
to think on this some more and we'd talk about it
again soon.

I really hope we do.

Signed: The future Dr. Fritz

CHAPTER 24

*I*f you're feeling any weakness or numbness in your arms or legs, it could be a bone spur," Fritz is telling Bertie.

It's an unseasonably warm day, the first of a week of them, the weatherman reports, with no rain in sight. The Burger Den has fans in every window. Aggie's perched on the back of the booth, an inch from a fan, wings up, feathers billowing. Since her pet store days, she's grown a glossy coat. My eyes dart over her. It's obvious not a feather is missing. Even the ones perpetually askew at the top of her head look somehow more put together. "Alastair," Aggie calls down to me.

I'm in my carrier. I was allowed out for a second there.

But then I tried to bite Fritz. I'm in time-out.

"Yeah?" I answer.

"I really love this, you know."

"Love what?" I ask.

"This. All of it. I love seeing you every week. I love Fritz and Bertie. I love bone spurs—"

"Aggie," I cut her off. "This—this isn't ideal at all. I mean, it was far from ideal when we lived at Pete's! We see each other, what—once a week? For two hours, tops? And even then we're shouting over the sounds of sizzling patties and 'Order up! Got a Big Bear burger with cheese!'"

"Oh, Alastair—" Aggie begins.

"No, Aggie," I say. "I mean it. This was not in the plan."

Aggie cocks her head. "What plan was that?" she asks innocently.

"What plan!" It comes out gruffer than I intended. I soften my tone. "What plan? The plan to break out of here. You and me. The plan to fly off, find a nice place to live? Remember Key West? Our palm tree? That plan?"

Aggie smiles weakly. "I thought those were stories," she says. "They were really nice stories. They made me feel better when I was sick."

"No," I say, feeling a little insulted. "They weren't stories. They were plans."

"Oh."

Stunned, I wonder now if some of my earlier plots could have worked. If maybe—had Aggie believed, had she truly believed—things could have been different. Maybe she would've walked out of Pete's faster. Maybe she *let* herself be caught by Fritz. The thought sends a shiver to the end of each feather I have left. I feel one let go and watch it drift out of my carrier and across the floor to the other side of the restaurant, nudged by the blowing fans.

Aggie clears her throat. "I'm sorry, Alastair. I just thought they were stories. I thought—I thought—I don't know what I thought. Melting store windows, finding mates in the wild—I've never really seen one of our kind out our window, you know. Then flying to some palm tree when we've never even learned to fly properly. I thought, well, they just seemed impractical—"

"Impractical! I'm nothing *but* practical!" I blurt out. "I almost busted us out once! I'll do it again. You'll see!"

"Okay, Alastair," she says quietly. "You're right. I'm sorry."

I feel another feather leave my body, watch as it turns and flutters across the room.

Fritz, who's gotten up to ask for a bottle of ketchup, takes no notice as it floats in a circle around him and gently lands at his feet.

It takes only seconds before it's trampled under-foot.

"I've got a plan," I say, trying to untangle the irritation from my voice. I relay it all. My foolproof scheme. From Fritz's bicycle bell to the bike basket.

I take a deep breath. "I'm executing it tonight."

Aggie looks worried. "Um, I'm not so sure, Alastair. I mean, what if something happens? What if you hurt yourself trying to fly out the window? Have you had flying lessons? What if Fritz leaves without you somehow, and—and you get left outside *forever*?"

"First of all, I'm part bird." It's an important distinction. "And birds fly, simple as that. It'll be fine, Ag. I promise. I've got it all under control."

"But what about Bertie?"

I wince. I've thought about this. I have. Bertie has sashayed across my mind a number of times as I've been working all this out. Or maybe it's just that she's always sashaying through rooms while I'm plotting, eating, composing poetry, scowling. It's just that there's nothing I can do. No use dwelling on it.

"Bertie's got Humpty," I tell Aggie. "And—Tiger. She'll be all right."

"That's not what I mean—"

"Two Grizzly grits and an orange Fizzy Pop!" the cashier's voice cuts in.

And that's it right there. It's always interruptions, always distractions. *That's* why I'm doing this. For me and my sister.

"Ag," I say, "I know what I'm doing."

I try to reassure her, but nothing seems to work. Aggie spends the rest of the meal silent and still while Fritz convinces Bertie to join him at his Pet Pals pizza fund-raiser at school and Bertie talks of shutting down her senior social for lack of interest. As they're packing up to leave, Aggie leans over and whispers to me.

"Maybe you're right, Alastair," she says. "I love you—you know I do—and I'd love to be together all the time again. But, well, don't you think it's risky? Maybe it's nothing, but Fritz told me about a parakeet that escaped from the shop once, and he was never right again after they caught him. In the head! And on top of that—"

"Order of fries and a Bear Cub box!" shouts the cashier.

"Aggie," I say soothingly, "it's going to be fine. It's all going to be fine."

Bertie picks up my cage, crosses the restaurant, and opens the door to the sidewalk.

"Tomorrow!" I shout to my sister. "I'll see you tomorrow!"

"Chicken wings!" shouts a kid in a poultry costume outside. "Get your chicken wings here!"

I look back as Aggie shudders.

"Oh!"

That evening Bertie's propped against her pillows in curlers, wiping her eyes and reading one of Everett's old poetry books.

"Oh, Alastair," she says, shaking her head. "This poem."

I'm over by the window checking things for tonight. Bertie hoists herself out of the sofa cushions and comes over to me, book in hand. She kneels so we're eye to eye. "'I know why the caged bird beats his wing,'" she recites. "I know why, Alastair! It says right here in the poem!"

She looks down at the page and reads slowly. "'A pain still throbs in the old, old scars.'"

Bertie waggles the open book, and the pages rustle. "It's right here, look! Your wing is bruised and you're beating against your bars, and all you're really doing is just saying your prayers to be free of all that hurt." She rests her elbows on the window-sill and sighs. "Pain still throbs in our old, old scars. Doesn't it? And here we all are just beating our wings. I think you could've written the poem yourself," she says to me.

I shake the words off. Fluff out my feathers. I've got a few left.

"You really could've written it, you know."

Well, I might've once upon a time. But I didn't.

And right now I'm too busy.

I turn my back on her.

"Oh, Alastair. Still fighting me." Bertie sighs again, and I hear her get up to turn on the kettle, hear two mugs being plucked from the tree. She tuts from the other room.

"What did you say, Everett?" I hear her ask, but she answers herself a few seconds later.

"Stubborn? I'd say dogged as a dandelion."

Tea for Two

It is planted
in the middle of the table.

A tree.

Anchored
by lace doily roots
speckled with years
of peppermint
lemongrass
chamomile.

It stands:
one trunk
four limbs
a single leaf dangling
from the end of each branch
heavy and glossed.

And every night it is
autumn.

THE SIMPLE ART OF FLYING

Leaves take flight
settle
on tattered ground
to take root, fill.

Four cupped leaves.

Sometimes with dew (for the bird)
Sometimes milk (for the cat)
And two
always

With tea.

But only three ever sit
beneath winter-scorned branches
sipping

dew
milk
tea

And one remains a ghost—
memories of the way things used to be.

CHAPTER 25

At the crack of dawn the next morning, I am ready and waiting.

I couldn't sleep. I spent half the night listening to the clock in the hall tick and the other half composing a—well, a poem.

Anyway.

I couldn't have asked for better conditions. Tiger woke Bertie six times last night, and each time she stumbled to the window and flung open the sash. Both cat and owner are snoring in the bedroom now. When I go to wake Bertie with my perfectly executed meow (I've been practicing), she should be groggy enough not to notice Tiger asleep on his kitty cushion. And while the sun came up a short while ago, a sheet of gray cloud has settled over it, threatening to storm and throwing the whole curtain-drawn apartment into midnight.

I'm safely tucked into the curtain folds next to the window (the one perk of having no tail feathers being there's less of me to hide). Been here about an hour now. Getting here wasn't too bad. I managed to elude caging last night by running from Bertie and hiding under the sofa. I may have had to nip her hand when she reached under to get me, though. When I did, she jumped and stared under the sagging cushions for a moment. She looked hurt.

But I can't think about that.

My stomach is swimming. Feels like I ate a mealworm.

It's nearly time.

Within minutes I hear the chime of Fritz's bell in the distance. Then another chime. And another. The next bell will be the one at our building's doorstep. From the moment it rings, I've given myself exactly fifteen minutes to escape and get safely into Fritz's bike basket without him seeing me.

I wait for it.

And wait.

And wait.

No bell. I feel panic bubble in my belly, begin to tickle my throat.

Where is it? He should've rung the bell by now. He should be on the second floor already.

Five minutes go by.

Ten.

Twelve.

Just then I hear a crash in the stairwell, and the *thump, thump, thump* of several dozen newspapers flopping down the steps like fish out of water.

"Oh *sickle cells!*"

I hear it, muffled, but I hear it. Fritz is in the third-floor stairwell after finishing up on the floor above, and he's dropped his bag.

I quickly count: three minutes left of the original fifteen, plus the other two minutes, twenty-three seconds it will take for him to pick up all the papers.

I will have to escape and get to safety in five minutes, twenty-three seconds.

Less, maybe.

It will have to be enough.

CHAPTER 26

*M*eow.
Meow.
MEOW.

I hear the comforter rustle on Bertie's bed. And then nothing.

Meow.

MEOW!

The blanket is thrown back, and the bed groans. Bertie gives a groan of her own. "I'm coming, you wicked cat," she says, her voice scratchy and thick with sleep. I hear the scuffle of her slippers on the kitchen linoleum and their whisper through the carpet.

Thunk. Bertie kicks the ottoman. "Ooooch!" she squeals.

Through the gauzy curtain, I see her slide the ottoman out of the way. She sits on it and rubs her toe. "You really try an old lady's patience, you know that?" she says, and stands.

I feel the blood thumping through my veins; I hear it in my earholes. The tips of my wings tingle, and my toes grip the sill harder to keep from falling over.

Bertie shuffles up to the window. "Where are you now, you darn cat? Change your mind?" She turns the lock and slides the glass up.

Fast as lightning, I'm out of my hiding spot and at the open window.

In the space of a second, I scan the street. Fritz's bicycle is propped against the railing, bike basket— looks empty?

I hear Fritz thumping on the stairs, heavy footfalls echoing through the building. He's on his way down.

I step over the threshold and past the dandelions.

"Wha—? Nooooo!" I hear Bertie shout, and feel the air rush behind me.

I fling wide my naked wings and jump.

Something catches me around the leg, and I look back to see Bertie, holding on for dear life. "Oh! Oh!" she exclaims, as I thrash with all my might.

Our eyes meet. Seconds disappear like a wave in the ocean. I continue to fight, but all sound is sucked away, as though the ocean inhaled and forgot to breathe out. Tears well in the bright blue of Bertie's eyes.

A familiar spark of pain flares through the old wing and lights a small fire in my chest. It burns. Right around the heart area.

I ignore it.

Bertie's eyebrows crimp, and she looks at me with watery eyes. Her words come out in a choking whisper. "Maybe I should—Henry did. And if he can, Bertie—"

She spots a dandelion, and her lips form a thin line, and a look of determination crosses her face.

"If that little thing's gonna fight so dogged hard . . . I'm not gonna get in his way. . . ."

And she lets go.

PART IV

20,000 FLIES UNDER the BED

—or—

To kill a PARROT-BIRD

CHAPTER 27

*A*ggie was right.

It could've turned out differently. Seeing as how the first part of my plan hit a few snags, the final outcome could've been a little hairy. Or worse. Might've been hairy as a sheepdog.

But it wasn't.

It was hairless. A Chinese Crested, if you're following the analogy. A hairless Xoloitzcuintli (yes, that's a breed, and no, I can't pronounce it for you). The plan was executed to perfection.

The plan *worked*.

Bertie never saw me walk to Fritz's bike, just

watched me float to the ground. (Okay, I sort of rolled down the fire escape. And then the *trush*— that fine, leafy portmanteau—broke most of my fall.) She'd popped her head back inside the apartment once I'd made it safely to the pavement.

Fritz never saw me climb his bike, flip open the basket lid, and settle myself inside. I even had time to spare. (The "*Gallstones and goiters!* Not again!" I heard him yell from the stairwell might have had something to do with it.)

By late morning I was safely parked under the elm in Fritz's front yard. By sundown I was choosing the right window (just needed to find the one with the PARROT CROSSING stickers) and climbing the flowered trellis straight to it. By the time Fritz was dreaming of tumors and typhoid, I was triumphantly crossing the finish line.

I squeeze through the scratchy wires of Fritz's broken screen and find myself in a darkened room. Posters are pasted everywhere. There's one of the circulatory system and one of the inner ear. A pair of lungs are stuck to the ceiling. In the dimness, I can spot a sleeping Fritz in bed, a desk, and two shadowy aquariums on the floor. It's too dark to see what's living inside.

Our old cage hunkers like an iron beast in the corner. I make a beeline for it.

"*Psst,*" I say as I peel back a corner of the blanket covering the cage. "Hey, Aggie! What'd I tell you? I made it! And not a feather out of pla—well, you know what I mean. Aggie?"

The cage is empty.

"Aggie?" I whisper it again into the cold steel skeleton; the sound of my voice rattles the bones.

Panic begins to sink its claws into my chest. I feel the air go out of me.

Aggie would never sleep outside our old cage. It's her *home.* She'd spent hours every day decorating it, mulling over where to place her toys, chewing wooden blocks into art. She'd never spent a night outside its bars. Never.

I pop back under the blanket and scan the room. Fritz's chest moves up and down under his sheet, but nothing else moves, nothing breathes.

Except whatever's in the aquarium.

My mind begins to form possible conclusions:

- Aggie's gotten an allergy to metal and prefers the cool, antiseptic quality of glass—no;
- Aggie's been traded in for whatever's behind the glass—not remotely likely, *partner*;
- Aggie's sick, and Fritz is keeping her close to the bed, where he can keep a better eye on her—possible;
- Aggie's held captive by whatever's lurking in the aquarium—and what *is* lurking in that aquarium?

Two words thump into my head from out of nowhere: snake bait.

I feel my feathers stand on end, and my heart thumps louder and faster, each beat a mantra of *snake bait, snake bait, snake bait*. I leave the cage and dart across the floor. In the middle of the room I trip over a pencil, and it goes skittering across the floorboards.

I freeze. Above me, Fritz snorts in his sleep. "My diagnosis is fatty liver," he moans. He turns over and begins to snore.

I take a step toward the aquarium, and the moment I do, something slithers out from under the bed. It's long and snakelike and . . .

"Alastair?"

Aggie. She steps out from the dark cave of the bed pushing a long, dirty, Fritz sock. "*There* you are! I was just doing some straightening. Had to clean out a few things under here—you'd be surprised how many socks get lost under beds."

I run to her and throw my wings around her. "Aggie—you don't know how—"

"How you made it?" she interrupts. "Yeah I do. Just like you said you would. I could see it in your eyes yesterday—I knew you'd be here, knew there was nothing stopping you. You're my brother. You're the strongest bird I know."

I'm feeling about as strong as a goldfish floater right now.

"Anyway," Aggie says, "I figured I'd get the place ready for you. I thought you'd need a good hiding spot, and under the bed is perfect. Fritz never looks under there—well, up until a few hours ago." Aggie's shoulders sink. "I had to try to keep Fritz from putting me away in my cage last night. I—I got the idea from you. I hid under the bed. Fritz didn't want to give up, though." She suddenly looks sadder than I've ever seen her.

"You okay, Ag?" I ask.

She looks at me, and a tear glimmers in her eye. "Not really," she says. "I bit him. I bit Fritz. I feel so terrible." Her head drops to her chest as she adds, "We both cried."

I try to reassure her. "It's okay, Aggie," I say, but stop. There's nothing I can say. Everything sounds hollow, selfish. *Good job, you helped a bird out? Eh, Fritz's finger will be fine . . . so, show me around the place! Feathers over fingers, blood before buds—a bird's gotta do what a bird's gotta do.*

I've got no problem saying these things to myself—but to Aggie? She's a different bird. She's . . . kind. Instead I say the only thing there is to say.

"I'm sorry, Aggie."

"It's okay," she says, but the sad note hasn't left her voice. "I'll be a better partner tomorrow."

Aggie grabs the sock she's collected from under the bed and carries it to a teeming, sock-filled fishbowl like the one Fritz had for her at Pete's, then pulls off the blanket and climbs up her cage on the far side of the room. "I think Fritz will be happy I found forty-one socks under the bed. I also found an old cholera pamphlet all crumpled up. He'll like that," she says. She reaches her open cage door and turns before going inside. "I left some of my food under there for you. I dropped it out of my cage all day, and it's not even the stuff I pre-chewed. That's how you'll be able to eat, I figure."

I'm surprised. I hadn't even thought about how I'd eat once I got here.

"Anyway, I'll be up here if you need me. Fritz shouldn't find me under the bed when he wakes up—he'd find you, too."

I watch as she climbs inside, fluffs her feathers a few times, and closes her eyes.

"Thanks, Ag," I say, grateful for her in a million different ways. Grateful in new and unexpected ways.

"Oh, you're welcome."

Her sleepy voice slips through the dark like a firefly. "Oh—and Alastair?" she says. "Porky was beside himself when I told him you were coming to stay for a bit. He and Tuna moved into the aquarium next to the bed last week. He says you two can resume those nightly poker games. Just thought you should know."

I guess it wasn't a snake after all.

CHAPTER 28

Aggie's set me up in a cozy, if dusty, corner under the bed, hidden by an old microscope box and a stack of Fritz's old, discarded picture books. There's a rumpled shirt, which I assume has been left as some sort of nest for me, an old bird dish for food, and one of Aggie's gnawed wooden art pieces. She's even left a book I remember Fritz reading to us, *Medical Poems for the Sick at Heart*, as a substitute for my old Norton. I just tasted a few pages. It was a cross between antiseptic and rot.

The next morning when Fritz leaves for his paper route, taking Aggie with him this time, I get my first chance to get out and take a look around.

"Hey there, old buddy!" shouts Porky as soon as I emerge. He does a double take when he sees me, but I try to pretend like the whole fifteen-feather thing is fine.

"Hello, Porky," I reply. "Long time no see."

"You're darn tootin' long time no see! You been off a long while! Hey, Tuna!—uh, I mean, *dear*! You see who's here?"

I've been listening to Porky's missus counsel old Charles the newt through a midlife crisis all morning. How she knows he's in crisis, I don't know. He hasn't gotten a word in all morning.

"Hey, Alastair! Good to see you!" she calls, turning back to her charge.

Porky grins. "Heh-heh-heh. Honey of a guinea pig, isn't she? Fits right in here. Fritz's sister's sure taken a liking to her." He picks up a hard green food pellet and eyes it for a second before tossing it over his shoulder. He selects a carrot from his food dish instead and continues talking with his mouth full.

"Fritz—he's easy. Likes anything with a tail. But Fiona—always pegged her a cat lady. Seems the type."

"How's the pet shop?" I ask.

Porky whistles through his teeth, and bits of carrot spray the glass. "You missed a fine kettle of goldfish there. Boy, things got pretty weird there for a while."

"Oh?"

"Yes, sirree! Place was like *Port Luna Love* when I left! Gerbils pulled off a major coup—it was carnage, just carnage. Babs ran off with some wild rabbit—saw the guy skunkin' around the store windows for a week, didn't think anything of it. And remember those tarantulas you let out that once? Well, seems they got a taste for prison break after you gone off." He scratches his chin absentmindedly. "Yep. Left the place in Vinny's hands. Not sure about it, though—guy's a little soft. Don't think he's got the stomach for it."

He continues. "Never had a hankering to leave. Thought about life on the farm for a bit. Figured I'd live in the shop forever, though. Hate to say it, but I'm glad to be done with the place."

I stop chewing the sunflower seed Aggie managed

to fling across the room and under the bed before she left. "Wait, what? Weren't you puffing everyone up about getting adopted and finding homes?"

Porky laughs his low, wheezy laugh. "Yeah, that was me. But that's what the guy in charge does, right? Takes care of the people around him. Makes them feel good about what's ahead." He shakes his head. "I never was *sure* about it. Heard some stories in my day. Heard some good endings too, but you don't know about a thing unless you've lived it, right? Things can *look* real good, and they can look real bad. You gotta live it to know which is which."

He smiles wide. "But I gotta say, this whole home-and-owner thing? It's better than I thought."

I snort. Bertie's wasn't terrible, but I'll be darned if it isn't half as good as whatever plan I'll come up with for my sister and me next.

"Naw, it's true," says Porky. "Sure, the days don't look so different: You eat, sleep, fix your fur and squeal a bit, chat with the neighbors, and such. . . ."

"A dream," I mumble.

"That's not the dream part," says Porky, giving me a reproving look. He steps back, squints his eyes, and looks me up and down. "You know what the difference between you and your sister is?" he asks.

"Feathers?" I offer, half-serious.

"Naw," says Porky, shaking his head. "You think you got the short end of the perch. Always so sure everyone's plotting against you, always looking for some bird-brained notion of the perfect life. You talk in your sleep, you know."

At the mention of "bird-brained," I feel the few feathers I have left ruffle and prick with irritation.

"Gratitude!" shouts Porky. "Aggie's got gratitude! You can get hung up on all the things you don't have, or you can be thankful for what you do got. It's all in the way you eyeball it."

I stalk back under the bed. I do not need to be lectured by a guinea pig. But Porky calls after me, and I can't block out the sound of his voice.

"You gotta know when to stop looking for the next best, better thing! You gotta know when you got it good! Stop grabbing for something that'll always fly away from you and never let you catch it. Sometimes you gotta open your hand to what's right there for the taking!" He shouts louder as I get farther underneath. "Sometimes it looks shabby, but really, it's a doggone good gift, and you were just too stubborn to open it!"

Then, from his aquarium, he tosses one of his food pellets, and it rolls under the bed and stops at my feet.

"Open your hands, Alastair!"

I don't even have hands.

That night I dream I'm in the pet shop. Our old heat lamp shines on three eggs wrapped like gifts before me. I unwrap the first. Inside is an empty pie plate with a few scattered crumbs. I unwrap the second egg. Another pie plate, this one overflowing with bubbling cherry. Halfway through eating it I realize it's a Chocolate Cherry Crumble. I cough and gag as the chocolate begins to make me sick. I stumble to the last egg. Inside is another pie. Like the one Bertie made me. I eat the whole thing in one bite and then stare in horror as the empty pie plate turns into a giant chocolate palm tree . . . that proceeds to eat *me* in one bite.

Must've been a bad sunflower seed.

CHAPTER 29

A week goes by without our anticipated escape. (Fritz is annoyingly responsible about latching Aggie's cage.) I'm still floating, though, being so near to Aggie much of the time, but today she leaves with Fritz for school and his Pet Pals fund-raiser. Since she left, I've been anxious to hear how it went.

Bertie had said she'd be there with bells on. She beamed when Fritz told her about two teachers planning to get their dogs trained over the summer for next year. And when Fritz had said Aggie had been spending time with a fifth-grade class that had a classmate with cancer, she'd wiped a tear and said she wouldn't miss this day for the world. I can almost picture her, pocketbook beside her, that stray pink curler she always forgets at the back of her head.

Part of me—a very small part, of course—wonders how she is, and if she's okay.

Hours later, Fritz and Aggie return. I hear them downstairs, but it's dark before Fritz's heavy footfalls sound on the steps. He tromps into the room, opens and shuts Aggie's cage door. I hear him pour pellets and seed, then get water from the bathroom down the hall to fill her water dish. For the longest time neither say a word. The silence begins to grate on my nerves.

I wonder, did Bertie wear her "fancy dancing attire" (a.k.a. the boa)? I'm willing to bet she did. . . .

She didn't try to take over school announcements, did she? Soon as Bertie sees a microphone . . .

Was there jitterbugging during band today?

Just some things one likes to know. No real reason.

Eventually, the quiet is broken by the sound of Fritz turning on the glowing box to his favorite show.

The sound of Letizia Tortelloni's soothing voice fills the room.

"After we season, the next step is to sear the roast. This gives the meat a nice crust." Letizia goes through each step carefully. I listen as she checks the roast, takes its temperature, pulls it out to rest. I think of Bertie's roast, the one I made off with. Letizia copies every step, right down to the horseradish garnish Bertie used "to perk it up a bit."

Meanwhile, Aggie is silent. The only noises Fritz makes are the little *mmm*s and *ooh*s and *that looks good*s he says quietly to himself.

"Next up, we look to the fruits of the cherry tree!" the box blares.

Cherry trees. Even Letizia's got that crazy story.

"It's my crostada," says Letizia. "It's like your American pie, no? Like your cherry pie. Except we add the chocolate."

I wonder if it's like Bertie's Cherry Crumble.

Fritz yawns and snaps off the glowing box before the show ends. "I'm tired, aren't you?" he asks Aggie, who squawks a small reply.

I hear him open a drawer, and his hands rustle around inside. He changes his clothes and flops into bed, and the springs wail above me. He turns over a few times, each time sighing loudly. When the sheets stop rustling and the only sigh is that of a timid breeze through the trees, Fritz finally speaks.

"Weird, wasn't it, Aggie? That Mrs. Plopky wasn't there? It wasn't raining. She promised she wouldn't miss this time. . . ."

Aggie squawks sleepily in reply.

Fritz turns over again. "But that doesn't bother me as much as the other thing," he adds, and a new silence opens a dark chasm in the room. From the shelf above the newt aquarium, a cricket trapped in its container strikes up its fiddle, and I sit listening, waiting for the second part of that sentence.

What other thing? What could be so very bothersome?

Minutes later I get my answer.

"It's those newspapers outside her door," Fritz says, worry creeping into his voice. "She hasn't picked up her newspaper in a week."

FROM THE DESK OF
ALBERTINA PLOPKY

Medical Log, June 12

- Age: Same
- Weight: Same
- Height: Same
- Current status: Good

It's getting close to the Fourth of July—my favorite holiday—and my birthday. Mrs. Plopky and I are supposed to celebrate by going to the Burger Den just like me and Grandpa always did.

But I'm not sure where Mrs. Plopky is right now.

I've been thinking a lot about what she said about the whole Grandpa thing not being my fault, and how things happen that we can't do anything about, and about how life is like a pie.

I wanted to find out how to make a pie. Letizia Tortelloni had some recipes. I watched all those episodes.

"First, the dough! You mix! Gentle. Gentle, *mia*

patatina, my little potato. Too much and it's tough like meat! Now roll. Into the plate to bake. Now for the filling. Add your sugar, and yolk, and boil the milk. *Perfetto!*"

That's what the transcript said, anyway.

I've thought a lot about it. I think what Mrs. Plopky means is that life has ingredients and lots of steps. Ingredients can be things like your family and friends, or maybe your interests, maybe even your heart. And I think those steps are things like your past, your plans, even your mistakes. I think she's saying you put it all together and try to make a good dessert out of it. As best you can.

It's like what Letizia Tortelloni says: "Ah, you take a chance. You mix the anchovy with the cheese, the pistachio with the peas. Who knows what you get? You try."

I think Grandpa would've liked Mrs. Plopky.

I hope she gets back from wherever she went. I'd like to treat her to the Burger Den. And I don't even care about the Red, White, and Bear Bl-urger. (July Fourth is the only day they serve it. Ketchup, mayo, and grape jelly on a burger. It is so delicious.)

I mostly want to tell her thanks.

And make sure that she's okay.

Signed: A concerned citizen

PS One more concerning thing is this: all the food Aggie's wasting lately. I wouldn't mind so much—it's not like Aggie knows better than to throw stuff on the floor. But I think she must be eating more too. A lot more. But it seems like she's getting skinnier every day. I don't get it.

CHAPTER 30

One week turns into two, then three, now six, and still no sign of Bertie. Every time Aggie joins Fritz on his paper route, she comes home with some sort of update:

"Somebody put a box outside the door for her newspapers. There are forty-two of them inside. I counted."

"Fritz knocked on her door today, but no one answered."

"All the flowers in her window boxes have turned brown."

I tell Aggie she probably went to Florida to visit Henry. Now that she doesn't have to worry about me, she can travel. Tiger can fend for himself. And—

With no need to replace poop papers at the bottom of my cage, she probably stopped collecting her newspaper. Why bend over and pick things up when you could throw out your back? And—

Her eyes are as bad as Delores's. She probably doesn't realize the flowers dried up.

Aggie remains unconvinced.

But I can't consider alternatives.

Meanwhile, life under Fritz's bed has been going swimmingly. Well, sort of.

Okay, not at all.

I rarely get out because, with school out, Fritz doesn't leave the room for much more than his paper route in the morning and his newly reduced, once-a-week shift at Pete's. There's been talk of a new pet store in town that's stealing all the big-ticket customers.

To add to my frustration, my bad wing's been acting up ever since I rolled down Bertie's fire escape, and Fritz turns over about eight hundred times a night. I get mere minutes of sleep. And, not to be uncouth, but there's an issue with the lack of lavatory space under here. Things are starting to, uh . . . pile up. Also, I'm hungry. And not just for eating material other than Fritz's old picture books. I'm hungry for actual food.

It's not that Aggie hasn't thrown scads for me to hunt and gather. The problem is I don't often get to it before Fritz cleans it up, scolding Aggie for being unusually messy. What I *do* get is a smattering of pellets that have fortuitously rolled under the bed, some rubbery bits of apple, and leftover cucumber slime. And absolutely, positively, no, not one cherry.

There is only one thing worse than listening to the sound of your own growling stomach.

It's listening to Aggie's.

"You feeling okay there, Ag?" I ask.

"Oh, I'm okay. Just a little sleepy."

Fritz has left Aggie home the past two days. He doesn't take her on his paper route when it rains—only it's not raining. We've had nothing but sun-dappled July days with a whiff of a breeze—*perfetto*.

Not that I've seen them. Porky's keeping me up to snuff on things like the weather and how many carrot missiles have *not* made it under the bed.

Aggie puffs her feathers and hunches over on the perch. "I think I just need an extra nap today," she says. "I should be better after that. Just as soon as I get rid of this little cough."

And here we have a new problem.

Because ever since I landed safely under Fritz's bed, I've been plotting the next escape. It's not like I've been busy. Other than throwing together a few scavenger hunts for dead flies and admiring the dust bunnies, I've had plenty of time to plot. I've had ALL the time to plot.

I've thought about dropping Fritz's *From Acne to Zygomycosis: Every Medical Malady from A–Z* dictionary on his head and knocking him unconscious while Aggie and I shoot out the broken screen. Or . . .

Knotting Fritz's dirty socks together to make enough rope to tie him up (saving one to stuff in his mouth, of course) and flying out of Dodge. And . . .

Hypnotize him, scrape together a raft made of sticks, and steal into the sewer system to Key West.

Each plan seems as plausible as the next. No problems there. (And I think I've made some real progress on that latch.)

The problem is that cough. The frequent naps. The problem lies in the fact that with Aggie feeling the way she does, we both know she's not up to a daring escape just now.

Truthfully, *I'm* not sure *I'm* up for one: I've got about seven feathers to fly with, and my stomach sounds like a trash compactor.

If I'm being honest?

I'm a little tired of plotting. It's exhausting.

But who knows?

Couldn't be a sunflower seed I ate. I haven't had one in days.

FROM THE DESK OF

Albertina Plopky

CHAPTER 31

It's midmorning, and Fritz is snoozing away above me. He bought a new slide set yesterday and spent half the night muttering to his microscope about the dangers of uncooked meat. I'm trying to get a little shut-eye myself when I hear a shuffling sound nearby.

"Alastair?" Fritz must have left Aggie's cage door unlatched after he stumbled back in from delivering papers and refilled her dish.

"Yeah, Ag? Coming back for that cashew you sent over earlier? I saved it for you. I know they're your favorite."

"Alastair—now's our chance."

"Our chance for what, exactly?" I ask as Aggie steps into view. "You mean to raid the birdseed bin?"

Her eyes flash, and she draws her feathers tight against her. "No, Alastair! To escape."

Wait.

Fritz is sleeping. Aggie's here.

He didn't lock the cage.

I clear my throat.

"Escape?" The word hangs in the air like a glass bubble, fragile, and ready to shatter with the slightest wrong move.

Aggie cocks her head and looks at me with a funny expression on her face. "Yes, Alastair, escape! You know, the two of us? Get out of here like you've been planning, find that palm tree—I can decorate . . ." She turns and starts tottering toward the light just beyond the bed skirt. I swallow and find myself following, a little woozy suddenly.

"Fritz is fast asleep. I can always tell when he's sleeping deeply by the size of the puddle on his pillow," Aggie calls over her shoulder. "It's pretty big, so I think we're safe."

I turn each word over in my mind—*Fritz, asleep, puddle, safe*—but I can't seem to shake this sudden pother fuzzing up my brain. It's possible a dust bunny got stuck up there.

We tunnel through the books, Aggie in the lead. We take a left at the sneaker box and find our way to the boundary line of the box spring. Aggie bends over and picks up the corner of one of Fritz's socks. It's oddly lumpy. She dips under the bed skirt and starts pulling the sock across the room with her beak.

"I packed us some food for the trip," she says in a muffled voice. "Already raided the birdseed. I threw some of that papaya from breakfast in there too." From a small hole in the sock, tiny seeds spill one by one onto the floor and roll away as Aggie pulls.

"C'mon, Alastair! You coming?"

The dotted line of birdseed snakes away, and I follow it, but carefully. If this is an escape, then Aggie's unused to the careful attention needed in pulling one off. I pause to take a peek over at Fritz, now visible across the room. He's indeed asleep. Big puddle. Porky and the missus are napping too. The window's cracked open, the screen ripped wide and waiting, an inviting breeze just beyond.

"You coming, Alastair?" Aggie asks again.

I look down at the line of birdseed. And suddenly the dust bunnies clear.

That line. It's like a line on a treasure map. It points to freedom. To the future I've always wanted for Aggie. The future I've been planning almost my entire life. Since . . . since that other baby bird voice.

I shudder. Aggie's waiting. "Yes," I say. "Yes, I'm coming. Of course."

I catch up to her at the spot just below the window, and we survey the climb. It's not too far to the ledge, and there's a chair we can use to get there. I look down at the sock.

Hm.

Aggie places a foot on the chair, catches a bit of sock in her beak, and yanks. It slides, but as soon as she attempts to lift it, the sock doesn't budge. "Might need to lose the papaya," she says.

I hold my breath, and I try to nudge it with my

beak, but the sock's too heavy. Would be with even a small amount of seed. "I don't think we can—"

"No, no, we can do it, Alastair! Just need a little more beak muscle. Here, try to get your whole head into it."

I let Aggie direct me *this way, that way, just a little to the left,* but the sock is planted. All the tugging has widened the small hole to something less small. A hailstorm of seed scatters the sock's contents in every direction.

"It's okay, Ag," I say. "We can get along without it."

Aggie frowns. "I just wanted to be prepared, just in case. We've been so hungry. I didn't want to—" She shakes her head. "No, you're right. You're always right. You know how to take care of us." She looks at me and smiles.

I find I have to force one in return.

Without the sock, we quickly climb the rungs of the chair and clamber to the windowsill.

"One more look, okay?" Aggie asks when we get to the top. Her eyes drift over my shoulder toward the bed. "He's so cute when he sleeps, isn't he?" Her voice drops to a whisper. "I sure am gonna miss him—"

"Hey, watch your step."

Aggie's on the edge of the sill. A toe dangles off. She stumbles a little but secures a few claws in the wood. "Oh—oh, yeah. Watch the step."

She turns back toward the window where the mouth of the screen is stretched wide, and the blue sky is brilliant and rushing off in every direction for as far as the eye can see. "It's periwinkle-powder-bright, remember?"

"What is?"

"The sky, silly! Remember?" She coughs and steps through the screen and out onto the narrow ledge. "We know this sky! And we know trees, and foraging. . . ." Aggie flutters her wings and holds her head high.

I step out too and nod my head slowly. "Yeah— yes," I say. My heart is beating like a drum in my earholes. I feel my skin tingle, sparking with electricity. The feathers at the back of my neck—the ones I can't reach—lift and quiver.

"And the bluer the sky is, the closer you are to

home. That's what you said, right, Alastair? We'll know home when we find it."

I nod my head. This is what we need. This is how my sister stays safe. This is how nothing bad ever happens again.

"Well, then—*jumpin' gingiva*, this is swell!" Aggie smiles and puffs her feathers. "Now what?"

I clear my throat. The problem with someone else hatching a plan is that you're left, well . . . winging it.

"Now we climb down this trellis," I say. "And then I—I—just have to check . . ."

I take in the placement of the vines, the strength of the lattice. I make sure I spot the rotted slats so we can avoid them on the way down. I check wind speed. I hurry up and calculate rental fees for our palm tree. (I hadn't thought about how many cherries per month seemed like an appropriate amount to charge those carrier pigeons.)

Meanwhile, Aggie's got her nose in the morning glories.

"Would you look at that! Look how fluttery these flowers are! I think I'll grab a few to decorate with. It'll feel just like home, don't you think? I mean, like *Fritz's* home." She coughs again and dips into the trellis below to pick a particularly delicate-looking specimen. "Ooh, this one's nice. Do you think we'll have a guest room? I always wanted a guest room. For when Porky, Tuna, and Fritz come visit—ooh, look at that one!"

"Careful, Aggie," I warn as she plucks another bloom. "Don't lose your balance—you don't know how to fly yet. Just—just give me a second—I'm—I just need to—"

To figure out where I saw a palm tree.

But Aggie's still eyeing the vine. "Don't worry, Alastair. I'll be careful. Besides, you already climbed this once. It's safe."

I'm about to argue, but before I can—

"Just one more," Aggie says, and leans over.

"Aggie, I mean it!"

"It's safe!"

All it takes is . . .

One tiny breath of wind.

A small stagger.

A bit of vine gives way.
I reach out to grab her—
I watch as she flaps
feathers catch
wings find air, claws find anchor.

But I lose balance.
   And fall. Grasp at leaves. Get a few.
   I dangle . . . a second.

But the branch lets go.

CHAPTER 32

They say your life flashes before your eyes in the final moments before you die.

And it does.

At least I think.

I mean, I *nearly* died. I fell a good two stories, and that's plenty of time to think.

To think about that sky, and how you thought you knew it, but once it was right there in front of you, it looked different than you thought. Bigger. Wider. More frightening. You never saw a blue more wild.

To think about home, and what that is, and who it's with. And where.

To think about your sister, and how she said

you knew how to take care of her, but how every time you tried, things didn't turn out the way you expected—how your provision seemed more like hunger, and your protection more like harm. And how the moment you stepped out on that ledge you realized you didn't even know where that palm tree was, and even if you did, could you climb it? Because without a feather, it's hard to fly.

You think about that tiny voice. The one you've tried so hard to forget. And how all along you've known:

There are some things you will always be powerless to save.

You think about these things as you're falling to your death.

But then . . .

You land in a kiddie pool Fiona's using for her current Choreography of a Tadpole project.

And you live.

I climb the trellis to Fritz's room for the second time in weeks, this time a little dazed and badly bruised.

It's different this time, and it's not just the bruises.
In fact, it's all different now.

The first time I climbed to try to break my sister out.

This time I climb to try to make her stay.

CHAPTER 33

It was a tiresome process. Climbing was one thing. But answering Aggie's questions as she shouted them from the windowsill was another.

"You sure you're okay?"

"Do you see the twenty-seventh flower to your left? There's a strong branch there!"

"Should you take a break? Maybe stop and smell the morning glories?"

Some things never change.

I wish you could have more of a say in which ones did.

Because it was the answers to the other questions she asked that I would have given anything to alter.

"Why don't I climb down?"

"Aren't we leaving anyway?"

"Don't you want me to come to you?"

Want?

I could eat a thousand dictionaries and never be able to explain this *want* to you.

How do you leave?

How do you say good-bye?

How do you let go?

I'm fairly certain there's no parrot manual for it. And even if there were, could you trust what it said? Who can say how to break your own heart?

This is what I'm thinking about as I reach the top.

Aggie steals back through the screen, and I have one toe inside, when Fiona hurtles through Fritz's door, waving an envelope. She is breathless and pale.

"Fritzerola!" Fiona screeches. "Look! It's your Mrs. Plopky! She sent you a letter!"

I freeze.

Fritz startles out of sleep with a snort. "Mrs.

Plopky? Really?" He wipes a stream of drool from his chin. "I thought she was . . . I thought the worst!"

Bertie.

Aggie.

Aggie, Bertie.

My mind is a jumble, but somehow both Aggie and I have the sense in that moment to back away from the window so as not to be seen loitering around the escape hatch.

"I can't believe it!" I hear Fritz say as he tears the envelope and snaps open the pages. "Mrs. Plopky— she's okay."

I feel a small bud of hope take shape. Maybe . . .

"Alastair got away, and she broke a hip!" Fritz cries.

The bud shrivels.

"Aggie?" I whisper.

"Yeah?"

"You need to get back to your cage now."

"But I can slip out as soon as their backs are turned. I can hold really still."

"No, Ag—"

"No, but I can! Fritz and I play statues sometimes. I always win!"

"No!" The word has more force than I intended.
Inside, I hear Fritz scamper out of bed, hear the
papers rustle. "No, Aggie," I say again, soft as I can
get it. "It—it's too dangerous. You're better off here.
I won't keep—the plan, it just didn't work."

"But—"

"Just get back to your cage. I won't go before—
just, get back in your cage."

"But—"

"Go!"

I've got a leaf in my ear, but I can see Fritz next
to the bed. He can't spot me. It helps that the pinky-
gray-plucked-turkey shade of my skin matches the
house's siding. I cannot see my sister, but I listen as
she slowly walks away.

"Yes—here," says Fritz. "She says Alastair got
away, out the window! Oh Mylanta. She says she
watched him go, but that she was going to go outside to keep an eye on him and make sure he was
safe—so she'd be there if he wanted to come back.

But she says she tripped over her ottoman—oh no—oh, but that just slowed her down. She says she put on her shoes, but it took a while to find them because she didn't have her glasses, and then she—oh!—she slipped on the tricky step and fell! She said it must have been right after I delivered her paper, because she'd seen hers outside her door, but when she—*Fiona*! She called my name! But I wasn't there!"

Fritz sinks to the mattress and groans. "I think," he says, "I think I need my paper bag."

Fiona flings open a drawer in his desk, and I watch as she rummages through it. "Here," she says at last, and hands it over.

Fritz puts the open bag to his mouth and breathes deeply a few times. "Thanks," he says when finished. "I'm prone to hyperventilation in times like—like—I'm just so sad."

Fiona's quiet. She sits on the bed next to Fritz. Their feet dangle off the edge. "Do you want me to read you the rest of your letter?" she asks.

"No," says Fritz. "I think I need to do this alone."

"You sure?"

"Yes," he answers. "I'd like to read it alone."

Fiona leaves the room, and Fritz turns over the page. He is quiet. From time to time, he clears his throat and makes little whimpering sounds. Finally, I see him spread the letter on his comforter and lie back in the bed, springs wheezing with every movement.

I haven't breathed. Fritz's words ring in my ears: *Alastair got away . . . make sure he was safe . . . slipped . . . broke a hip.*

I feel one of my last feathers slip from my body and realize—I'm holding it in my beak. I tore it out.

And I don't even care.

I'm a feather picker, okay? Through and through.

"Fiona!" Fritz shouts all of a sudden. He leaps out of bed, and the springs howl. I hear him clatter about, fiddling with Aggie's cage—she must have managed to slip back inside.

"Fiona!" Fritz shouts again. "Get your flower-power flip-flops on! We're going to see Mrs. Plopky!"

Aggie's harness snaps.

"Prickly Pines Retirement Village, here we come!"

* * *

They leave in a flurry of papers and Ocean Air Armpit Spray. I watch as the leaves of Bertie's letter flutter to the ground.

When all is quiet, I creep back through the window. Fritz and Aggie are gone, but something makes me want to stay hidden, to crawl back into my dark under-bed lair and let it swallow me whole.

"Hey there, buddy!"

Porky's been waiting. Of course he has.

"Heck of a day, eh?" He doesn't wait for an answer. "Seems we were taking a snoozer during all the commotion. Tuna heard about everything from the newt."

Porky whistles through his teeth. "Gee whiz. Couldn't believe my ears just now when she said the two of you tried to escape. Looks as if it turned out all right in the end, though, didn't it? Tucked in like a turtle! Safe and sound now, aren't yeh?" He winks at me, his toothy smile bright.

"Safe and sound," I repeat. "Sure."

"Always comes right in the end! You did good, kid. It was right coming back like you did. We all need looking after here."

Little does he know I'll still be leaving. Alone.

Porky reclines in the corner of his aquarium and puts his feet up on the edge of his food bowl. "Yep—we all need a little looking after. Someone to scratch our backs. And Fritz—he ain't too shabby! Heck of a back scratcher he is, heck of a back scratcher. A true friend, that one. A *rare-a avish*, or whatever he likes to say."

He trails off for a second as he eyes a bit of celery, sniffs it, and takes a bite. "There's no use escaping, I always say, if you got an owner like that. The cedar shavings on the other side of the glass aren't any cleaner, know what I mean?"

Not so much.

But Porky falls silent, and I make my way under the bed one last time, left to my thoughts. Only now, I'm thinking about cedar shavings.

What *will* that other side of the glass look like? Not shavings. Pine needles? Palm fronds, if I can find them? Or will I be shacking up with an abandoned hedgehog or two living under someone's back stairwell? I wonder. Where does a sisterless or ownerless soul go?

Ownerless.

Bertie.

I can see Bertie flouncing across the apartment in her boa. Bertie at teatime. I think about the gift of Everett's old poetry books and her cherry pie. I think of Bertie's constant chatter and her laughter and remember the empty gymnasium and her tears. I think about a bowl filled with pits, and how she said nothing about it. Just filled it right back up with cherries and gave it to me.

I think of the broken hip.

There's really nothing I don't break.

Medical Log, August 1

· Everything: AMAZING!

You'll never believe it, Official Medical Log.

Fiona and I went to see Mrs. Plopky today.

I didn't think I was ever going to see her again, and KA-BLOOEY! Today I got a letter, and she's okay after all.

She's been down at the Prickly Pines. I walked right past her window this morning and never even knew it! She never transferred her newspaper subscription because she didn't feel like reading it for a while. She said she had some thinking to do before she saw me again and gave me any more advice. She saw me delivering papers once. But instead of saying hi, she just said a little prayer right there while she was soaking her teeth.

Jiminy rickets, life is funny sometimes.

Me and Fiona and Mrs. Plopky, we talked for a while. We talked about Mrs. Plopky's hip and how it was the pits. About Aggie and Alastair. About her friend Irma looking after Mrs. Plopky's pets for her, and how Irma likes to put doll bonnets on the cat. We even talked about Grandpa.

Fiona had a lot to say about Grandpa too. That was another thing I never knew. I didn't know Fiona was still so sad, and that sometimes it's hard for her to make friends because she's scared she's going to lose them. She's scared of her heart hurting. Mrs. Plopky said you don't throw out a cherry because you know there's a pit. She said that you take the pits as they come, and not before. I liked that.

Mrs. Plopky took us on a tour. She's got a pool, a ballroom to dance in, a library, and nice gardens all around. And we met lots of her friends. A few pinched my cheek and said, "What a nice young man!" but I didn't mind. I even met Mrs. Plopky's doctor. He showed me her hip X-rays and gave me a book on shingles since he had an extra copy.

It was like the best day ever.

Signed: Doc Feldman

CHAPTER 34

That night after they get back, Fritz and Fiona scurry back and forth, gathering sheets and blankets to set up a tent in Fiona's room. Fritz brings a textbook to study how to set a broken hip and another for Fiona on geriatric exercise regimens.

Fiona's thinking of starting a water-aerobics class at the Pines.

I've got my ears pricked for talk of Bertie, but I get nothing. I listen to them read off interesting facts from their books and tell old Grandpa stories, like the time a giraffe at the zoo licked an ice cream cone right out of his hand. They laugh into the deepest hours of morning.

When it gets quiet, and I'm certain they've drifted off, I tiptoe out of my hiding spot.

This is it. It has to be. Time to say good-bye.

Aggie pipes up from her cage. "Cherry for your thoughts."

I didn't realize she was still awake.

Her voice sounds sleepy and sad. "Well, except I don't have a cherry . . . I could give you a cashew, though."

I manage a half smile and scrabble through the handful of grimy, tea-colored socks Fritz has left on the floor for Aggie. Aggie, who loves to throw Fritz's dirty socks in her basket. Aggie, who's said she's just a little tired lately and will get to it later. Aggie, who's lost a few feathers, looked a little ill, said nothing of her hungry belly, and given me more than half of her food now for weeks. That Aggie. My sister.

I climb the rungs of the cage until the two of us are face-to-face.

"I'm no good at looking out for you," I tell her. I feel the shame rise in my cheeks. Even parrots blush.

"That's not true!" Aggie says.

"Yes, it is."

Aggie gets quiet. After a little while, she clears her throat. "I know," she says, not unkindly. "But you're a great brother."

"You would've been better off with a gerbil."

Aggie looks shocked. "Oh, but you are! You just didn't know we couldn't do it on our own—"

"Ag—" I don't want to talk about all the ways I didn't take care of her. "Ag, I'm sorry. For stealing your food, for trying to make you escape—for everything. I'm going to fix it. Here, Fritz—he's your home, Aggie. *This* is how I take care of you."

"*This?*"

"Leaving." My breath catches. "I'm leaving, Aggie. A home is all I ever wanted for you, and you've got one, and—and maybe I did too, but—well—I can leave you here, and you'll be okay. You'll be safe. Fritz will take care of you just like Bertie took care of me, and—"

"*Leaving?*" Her eyes widen. "But you can't leave! Where would you go? How will I see you?"

"I don't know, Ag. But I can't stay here. You need

to eat, and—and you know Fritz wouldn't keep me. He'd try taking me back or someth—"

"Yes. Oh, yes! That's it, Alastair!" Aggie's face softens.

"What's it?"

"You can go back to Bertie!"

Oh, my sister. My sweet sister. She'll never stop looking for that good spot on a bad apple.

Even if it's moldered to the core.

I think I'm going to miss that most.

"Aggie, I'm not going back to Bertie."

She shakes her head, hard. "No. What do you mean, Alastair? Of course you are. You have to! She's your rara avis. *A true friend is a rare bird*, remember? You need her!"

"Doesn't matter—"

"It does!" Aggie is angry; I can see it. "She'll take care of you! She—"

"She doesn't want me! I broke her! She's in the Prickly Pines because of me! And I almost broke you." I pat my sister with a stubby, still painful, still bent wing. "I've got to go, Ag. Please, just say good-bye. I love you, but please—just say good-bye."

Aggie's crying now. "But Bertie's okay now! And you didn't break me! I'm fine! I'm not too hungry! Stay! I love you. We can find a way. Love can do a great many things—just, please, just stay, we'll figure it out."

"It's not enough," I say.

And at that very moment, as if the Fates have a venomous sense of humor, Aggie's belly growls. Our eyes meet.

"See?" I say. "You can't *eat* love."

I turn and begin clambering down the cage to the floor.

"Please! Alastair!"

"Hey, yeah, Alastair," Porky interjects. He's obviously been listening. "Don't go. You two got love!"

But I am resolute. As always. As ever. Parrot-man of the wiser African grey sort. And this? It's the only wise thing I know.

This is it.

"Alastair!"

I walk across the room toward the gaping screen and its jagged teeth. As I get near, I find papers scattered on the floor beneath the chair. I step on one and realize it's Bertie's letter. Without thinking, I pick it up and taste it.

I should go. I *need* to go.

But that taste.

I can't help myself. (It's that self-control thing. Mine's always been lacking.)

I begin to rip and shred, tear and eat. Words fill my taste buds. Flavors deepen. Sentences and thoughts find their way to my head.

They burn a hole in my heart. . . .

Albertina Plopky

(CONTINUED)

My dear boy, it's just as I told you: Life is like a pie. And it's true. Life has got its main ingredients, its flavors, its spice. You can't go spoiling your pie because you missed a step or got the wrong ingredient. Too much of anything turns your pie into a pickle.

And in the end, if you got your recipe right, you get a mighty good dish out of it. And that's true too. And it's a good story. But I think I got one better.

It's like the old song goes:

"The sweet things in life, to you were
    just loaned . . .
Life is just a bowl of cherries."

That's something Alastair showed me, believe it or not. Life is just a bowl of cherries, and you enjoy every last one while you got 'em there in front of you. But one more thing—

You leave the pits.

Pits? They're all those things you don't like, all the things you can't control. Sometimes you got to set those pits aside.

And oh, dear boy, there are days it feels like everything is pits, that all you got is pits. And, Fritz? Sometimes that's closer to the truth than you might want to think about.

My life was all pits when my Everett died. Felt like pits when Henry moved away and I didn't get to talk to him every day. The years are full of pits. Sometimes you just got one, and sometimes you got a mouthful.

And it's okay to hang on to those pits for a while. Some take a while to work through. You got to chew on them a good bit before you can even think about doing something else. But don't you worry about it. Anything that's worth anything takes a bit of time, and some teeth.

Me? I've been chewing my pits for a long time. Some of them, maybe too long. Should've been remembering the taste of cherry, not cracking a tooth on the pit. Because, you know what I realized?

Pits are seeds.

Seeds can become trees.

Trees can fill your bowl and a hundred
others with new cherries—*different* cherries—
but sweet ones. But you got to spit.

So, eat your cherries, young Fritz.

And as best as you can, you sow those pits.

I've sown a few now. I never forgot that
strange night I went to the pet shop not so
long ago and walked out with a dead bird.
A dead baby bird! Now that I think of it, it
was right about the time our Alastair and
Aggie were born. Could've been a relative,
for all I know. I buried that little thing, and I
remember thinking it was like burying a seed. I
realize now, that's exactly what it was, because
I went home wishing for some company, and
sometime later, that seed found me living with
an unsightly imp of a parrot who ended up
bringing me a joy I hadn't felt in a long time.

When he flew off, I sowed my broken
hip in the Prickly Pines. And, oh, I wasn't
pleased to do so. Matter of fact, I didn't have
a choice. That pit was sown for me.

I could have dug it back up. I could have
taken my hip right out of there soon as the
doctors gave me the go. Could've popped
that pit back in my mouth and given it a
good chew. But I didn't.

I let it grow.

And that seed? It's becoming a tree for me.

Now, instead of traveling all over creation to visit my friends or make a thousand phone calls like I used to, Janet, Melly, and Joan and a whole place full of new people are just a door away. I got a company of sweetness around me—even Henry's talking about visiting more often to keep an eye on me.

Since I got here, I haven't once eaten supper alone.

It took one nasty pit, but now? My bowl of cherries feels like it's filling up. Who knows? Might even run over.

Because, who says bad things have to stay bad forever?

Who says bad times can never get good?

Yesterday isn't always, and neither is today, and if a little time and warmth and light can turn an ugly, old pit into a tree, who's to say a little time can't do the same for you? For me? I know what I'm betting on.

I'm betting on trees.

And that's what I hope for you, my boy. That your pits—all those worries about not being well-liked or worries about your health, embarrassment at having interests different from the other kids around you, feeling lonely and missing that father and grandfather of yours—that those pits will, in time, turn into trees for you. I can't promise it, but I hope they will. I hope they produce fruit, lots.

I pray you have more cherries than you know what to do with.

It's what I hope for that stubborn bird, too, wherever he is. I hope he finds that bowl of cherries he was looking for, and if not, well, I've got mine to share if he ever makes his way back. Spitting pits is a lot nicer when you've got someone to do it with.

You and Aggie and Fiona come visit me now. There's a pretty bench in the garden I got picked out for a picnic.

I'll bring the cherries.

Love,
Bertie Plopky

Bertie's letter, it's a poem, an epistle.

It tastes bitter and sweet. Tastes like sorrow and forgiveness. It has the acid taste of guilt and sadness, but I taste hope, too. And a relief that could only come from knowing where that little voice ended up, and how. I taste cherries and fruits I can't put my wingtip on, fruits I can only imagine.

It tastes the way I feel about Aggie.

I pray you have more cherries than you know what to do with.

It tastes like love.

True, some of it's a little suspect. I'm never going to believe something as perfect as a cherry tree exists. But still.

It's the best thing I've ever eaten.

"Aggie?"

"Yeah?" she answers, a hitch in her voice.

"I think I'm going back to Bertie . . . ," I say slowly. I turn and look at her. "Turns out, well, I guess you *can* eat love, after all. It's just a different kind of food."

She sniffles. "Like Letizia Tortelloni makes?"

I shake my head. "It's *like* a food. Just doesn't fill your stomach."

"It fills your heart?"

A lump gathers in my throat and threatens to

choke off my words. I let them tumble out before they're lost. "Yeah. It fills your heart. Get some sleep, Ag. Big day ahead."

We say our good-nights, and I find my spot under Fritz's bed. Again.

Only, this time I don't stay hidden. I stay just under the edge, where I can get a glimpse of my sister.

A cupful of moonlight spills across the wall above her cage and throws light over her feathers. She's already snoring.

Some things never change.

For now, I'll watch over her. I'll keep my eyes open for as long as I can.

I can sleep some other time.

CHAPTER 35

The sun pops its head over the horizon. I hear the purple martins and the sparrows cheer. Fritz comes to the room, lets Aggie out of her cage, and drops in a few crickets for Charles. Porky grunts happily as Fritz scratches him behind the ears, while Aggie makes her way under the bed, where I'm waiting.

"Do you have a plan?" she asks.

"I'm flying the coop," I say, an attempt at a joke.

"What?" There's fear in Aggie's eyes.

"Just escaping the bed, Ag. That's all."

She still looks worried. "But what made you change your mind?"

My eyes find the old partner poster tacked above

Fritz's desk (Fritz must've bought two, because I distinctly remember eating it). "It's you and Fritz. A bird and her boy." I clear my throat. "And Bertie needs me."

Aggie looks down at the floor and nods her head. "And you need Bertie, too, right?"

"Well, I—"

"Well, nothing," Aggie says. "It's true. You need Bertie just as much as she needs you. As much as I need Fritz."

I shake my head. "I can't believe I'm going to say I need a *human*."

"Who'd have thought you'd admit you weren't one?"

Good point.

"I think it's still up for debate—"

"Me," Aggie interrupts. "I knew. I knew from the beginning. You're the best and strongest bird I've ever known."

"Oh, Aggie," I say with a sigh. "Always seeing the peaches in a dish full of pellets. I'm definitely going to miss that most."

"Yeah," she says. "But there's no telling how

many amazingly wonderful things started from one good pit."

We step out into a little spotlight of sun: Aggie, feathered and as beautiful as I've ever seen her; me, plucked and naked as the day I was born. I make the sound of Bertie's old oven timer to get Fritz's attention. *"Tick, tick, tick—DING."*

Fritz turns, expecting to see what, I don't know, but his eyes fall on me. *"What in the blue bunions—"* He claps a hand over his mouth, stunned, and blinks a few times. Without warning, he begins to giggle uncontrollably.

Aggie throws a wing over my back and squeezes me close. I look at her, and she smiles.

"Well, *shiver me blisters*," says Fritz when he's finally gotten hold of himself. "It's Alastair."

That afternoon, the four of us—me, Aggie, Fritz, and Fiona—walk up the stone path to the tree-canopied bench Bertie's picked out as her favorite spot on the Prickly Pines grounds. A silver walker waits beside her, ready to help.

"We've brought you a surprise, Mrs. Plopky!" Fritz calls as we get near.

"Oh? Have you, dear?" Bertie replies, shading her eyes and squinting in the light. "Well, what is it? A pony? You know my eyes are bad."

Fritz pushes me forward and sets me in Bertie's lap. Bertie looks down and grins.

"Why, *there* you are!" she says when she sees me.

As if she was waiting on me all along.

Dear Delores,

You make a fine casserole.
I do a mean pie.
What do you say we start over?
Shall we say dinner at 4:30?
I'll wear my boa.
Got you one too.

Your friend,
Albertina K. Plopky,
1955 Susquehanna Prize-Pie-Baking Champion

PS I forgot how bad your eyes are till just now, and look how small I wrote up there! Well, just have Betty or Florence read this letter to you.

Unless you can find your magnifying glass.

CHAPTER 36

Bertie plunks herself on the bench. Two large pots of geraniums with a few stray dandelions squat in the sun nearby. I scoot from my perch on Bertie's walker onto the bench back, and a grassy breeze ruffles the fairly respectable coat of feathers I've managed to sprout since coming here ten months ago.

"Lovely, isn't it, Alastair?"

I squawk and flap my good wing.

"It's lovelier with you," says Bertie. "You're just the cherry on top."

I like that: the cherry on top.

We close our eyes. We've spent many an afternoon

after tea soaking in the sunshine, listening to the chanting of the *loppy crogs*, and napping. A little afternoon snooze in the spotty sun is good for mending broken hips and growing feathers . . . or so Fritz says.

I've just drifted off when something bops me on the head. I startle and look to see what it is, and to my utter shock I see a cherry rolling down the stone pavers. I look around quickly.

Aggie and Fritz?

I scan the horizon. There's nothing in sight but for a lone garter snake warming himself a little way off. *He* couldn't have thrown it. Snakes lack arms, of course.

I shake my head and close my eyes. Maybe it was my imagination. Or maybe Bertie had that cherry in her pocket, and it fell out.

Must've been a bug that ran into my head and flew off. A big one.

BOP.

Again! I open my eyes to see another cherry, this time coming to a stop in the pool of Bertie's skirt, its gleaming flesh fiery in the sun.

I look around again. The snake's not even there to blame it on this time. Nothing stirs, not for miles. Only the wind. And the flower petals. And the leaves . . .

. . . in the trees.

I swallow. I pinch my lids shut and tilt my head toward the sky.

I say a silent prayer . . .

And open my eyes.

More cherries than I know what to do with.

Medical Log, June 28

- Age: 22 years 11 months
- Weight: 187 lbs
- Height: Somewhere around 71 in
- Current status: Excellent; ingrown toenail long gone.

Found this old logbook as I was cleaning out my room before going back to school this fall. Thought I'd write one more entry, for old times' sake. Before I finally become an actual doctor, that is.

Harvard Medical School, here I come.

Signed: Fritz

Afterword
-or-
Rhyme of the Ancient Parroter

You don't always get what you want in this life.

    You can plan it all out, plan on flying away, eating poetry in your palm, but sometimes your wings are broken, and Key West's a little too far.

    And what you get is the Prickly Pines Retirement Village instead.

    And sometimes? It's not so bad.

    Sometimes you make friends with humans you never expected. Sometimes your feathers fill back in and you begin to look like the proud bird you always suspected you were— although a bit less proud, and a little more thoughtful. Sometimes you enjoy attending Pet Pals at the Pines and gnawing on the large library of books an old-folks home can amass. You might realize that the Pines probably has a better assortment of books than any palm tree ever could.

Sometimes the palm tree's the wrong ingredient for your pie.

The years will tick by, and as they do, life will bring you some surprises.

You might hear, one day, how that cat got what *you* always wanted, how Tiger's moved to the Key West you always dreamed of. There might be a slight sting at first, but it mellows. You might even find yourself wishing him well—something you never thought possible. And later, when you hear that it was Fiona who adopted him when Henry got her a job caring for Hemingway's roaming generations of six-toed cats, and that she's using him for a cats-ercize class, there will only be a hint of gloating. A mere hint.

But other surprises will knock you sideways.

Like how heartbroken you'll be when a Bertie flies on to that glittering city in the sky without you.

Or how grateful you'll be when your sister comes to stay with you and the residents of the Pines while Fritz is off at medical school.

You'll be shocked how happy you feel when that same Fritz specializes in geriatric

medicine and takes a job at none other
than the Prickly Pines Rehabilitation and
Retirement Village itself.

You might be surprised at how much you
appreciate having your own Fritz-made
perch on the medicine cart. You might find
yourself shouting *Oh, sickle cells!* every time
someone drops a bottle of pills, or when they
serve stroganoff for lunch. Crazier things do
happen. . . .

You don't always get everything you want
in this life.

But sometimes what you do get is better
than you imagined, better than what you
even thought possible.

Sometimes cherry trees do exist.
Imagine that.

—Alastair

Senses and Sensibility

You hatch
And you're still blind.
Light and shadow less vague,
I suppose.
But unlike your ears, which
have broken the surface and
beheld,
your vision remains
muffled.
You stumble over yourself,
over cotton hills and valleys alike,
and the prickly pinecone
of your sister,
wondering,
Is this life?
Is it all a blind bumbling
into the unknown?

And yet,
yet . . .
A deep knowing
flashes

in your ears, longing
screams
behind your eyes,
then just like that,
the curtain parts,
Act Two unfolds,
and you thank whatever
artist, that life saw fit
to paint sunrise

on a peach.

ACKNOWLEDGMENTS

This book was a winding eight-year, soul-searching journey. A crazy dream. A seed and, at times, a pit of one. It's not every day a pit grows roots, sprouts leaves, and gives fruit. But when it does, where do you begin in expressing gratitude to all the people who've tended that seed along the way?

First, a special thank you to:

My editors—Amy Cloud, who believed and championed that belief into a book, and Tricia Lin, who took the baton and ran with it. I'm ever grateful for your wisdom, grace, and hand-holding. And to the team at Aladdin—Mara Anastas, Cassie Malmo, Caitlin

Sweeny, Michelle Leo, Elizabeth Mims, Brian Luster, Karin Paprocki, Mike Rosamilia, Tiara Iandiorio, and Jennifer Weidman—a hearty thanks for coming alongside and for your tireless work and patient help.

To Rena Rossner, my steadfast agent. You're proof one e-mail can change your life. Thank you for seeing into the heart of this surly parrot and determining to get his voice heard. You're the one, the original, *the* Renegade.

To my Pitch Wars mentors, Amanda Rawson Hill and Cindy Baldwin. There aren't words enough to write. Alastair's, Bertie's, and Fritz's stories would be so much less, but for the two best and most passionate mentors on God's green earth. Your enormous hearts and tremendous giftedness enabled me. Thank you for all the hours, for your enthusiastic willingness to share your craft and revision know-how, for your endless support. (Thanks, too, for my education on the art of GIF communication.) You've taught me bucketfuls, heaped and spilling over. I'll never stop being amazed by you. I treasure your friendship, and I'm sorry, but you're stuck with me forever. My endless thanks, dear kindred spirits, to the moon and back. (Sorry for the overuse of adjectives here, but it was necessary.)

Warmest thanks to my writing community:

The Pitch Wars family. To Brenda Drake and all who continue to make this magic available to aspiring writers like me, and to the 2016 alumni. To the 2016 middle grade mentees in particular—our clubhouse is my favorite. And to my #teammascaratracks siblings, especially Kit Rosewater. I love being related to you. England awaits us. Kettle's on.

The Renegades. We make a great (and crazy) clan.

Thanks to the Novel Nineteens, particularly Julia Nobel, our fearless leader. I'm grateful to have a debut group like you. What generous hearts you have.

To my Western and Central New York SCBWI crew. And to my critique partners and friends—Kate Day, Ryan Howlett, and new recruit Brian Montanaro. Thank you, thank you. You've loved Alastair from the start.

This book wouldn't be what it is without inspiration, big and small, and support from the following people:

My grandmothers, Joan Kowalewski and Betty Campbell. Nonnie, thanks for baking that disastrous pie and serving it to your unsuspecting family. You're sweet as strawberry rhubarb—but hold the salt. And Gram, I love you a whole big batch.

My parents, Ron and Dr. Doris Campbell. I wouldn't have my Norton if you hadn't supported your book-loving daughter's decision to major in English. Many thanks. Mom, the menagerie of pets, the days we spent with you at work, and the veterinary exploits you regaled us with at the dinner table every night came in handy. Thanks for living big dreams first. And Dad, thank you for loving your family. You're our Everest.

My cheerleaders—Brenna Campbell, Jennie (and Craig) Campbell, Jen Scholz, Corry Tobben, Christine Fischer, Rachael Stahl, Jill Sweeney, and Sue Limpert. All these years you've prayed, you've held on to faith. Your friendships mean the world to me, and I love you with my whole heart. To all the Campbells, Leonardos, and Limperts, thanks for cheering me on and for being the greatest family ever known. And to the hundred others I could list. Every time you prayed a prayer, sent a note, even offered those seemingly small words of encouragement, it watered the seed. Every time I was tempted to quit, I remembered *you*.

Head cheerleader, Annie Bullard. I'm not sure I would have made it without you. Thank you for saving me from all the Mr. McGregors in the vegetable garden. I think my tail survived—intact—because of you.

My children, Caleb, Sam, and Amelia. You're the cherry on top, my heart, my everything. Thanks for letting your old mom chase her dreams and for never doubting they were within my reach. (And thanks for choking down all those chicken nuggets I said were dinner.)

My husband. Andy. Few would support their

unemployed dreamer of a spouse as fiercely and completely as you have done and continue to do. I love you.

And to the Author and Muse, the Seed-sower, Waterer, and Grower. This book has been, is, and will always be yours.

CHECK OUT THESE AMAZING BOOKS FROM

BARBARA DEE!

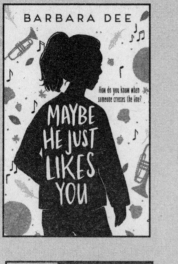

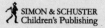